BREVITY & ECHO

Brevity & Echo

An Anthology of Short Short Stories

Edited by

Abigail Beckel and Kathleen Rooney

Rose Metal Press

2006

Rose Metal Press
P.O. Box 1956
Brookline, MA 02446
rosemetalpress@gmail.com
www.rosemetalpress.blogspot.com

Library of Congress Control Number: 2006938189

ISBN-13: 978-0-9789848-0-9
ISBN-10: 0-9789848-0-3

Book design by Rebecca Krzyzaniak.
See "A Note About the Type" for typeface information.

This book is manufactured in the United States of America and printed on acid-free paper.

TABLE OF CONTENTS

Rose Metal Press is grateful for the financial support of the following people, whose generosity made *Brevity & Echo* possible:

$1000 and above

Tom and Tania Beckel
Bill and Susan Harkins
David and Barbara Seay
In Memory of Jeanne Carenen Stalick
Gloria Wehr and Chris Hertz
Chris and Ann Wehr

$100 to $999

In Memory of Sarah M. Beckel
Nancy Lenihan Geltman
Mark Harkins
Matt and Olga Harkins
Nancy and Robert Leclaire
Sandra and Charles Longer
Wes and Lisa Markham
Jessica Palmer Kramer
Jessica Pantages and Jon Nielson
Stacey and Casey Rayburg
Richard and Mary Ann Rooney

Up to $100

George Awad
Annamarie Beckel
Katherine Beckel
Margaret and Dill Blackwell
Elizabeth Bruce
Joan Dobbie
Brooke Everley
Helen Kress
Pam and Joe Luppert
Beth Rooney and Nick Super
Megan R. Rooney
Cari and Brian Rotenberger
Kashi Sehgal
Carmen Stewart Jessup
Jeremy Wang-Iverson

The editors would also like to thank: Rebecca Krzyzaniak for many generous hours of design work; Rose Metal Press Board Members Alex Brown, Lisa Diercks, and Pamela Painter for their expertise and advice in printing, production, design, marketing, anthology compilation, and the literary landscape; Emerson College for its support of the project; Serge Bechade of Prince, Lobel, Glovsky, & Tye LLP for his guidance in all things legal; Martin Seay and Caryn Lazzuri for their help with naming the press and the book and for their administrative work throughout the book compilation and production process; and our families and friends for their love and their enthusiastic support of Rose Metal Press and *Brevity & Echo*.

Preface

THE EDITORS

This is a book of short short stories. Fitting, then, to have a short short intro. Were it to be distilled enough to put on a T-shirt,

READ SHORT,
THINK LONG.

is what it could say. Since we have a bit more space, though, we'll say this:

After months of planning, reading, selecting and arranging, Rose Metal Press is thrilled to present *Brevity & Echo: An Anthology of Short Short Stories.*

Why "brevity?" Because the stories are condensed, essential. Why "echo"? Because the stories bounce and resonate in your brain long after you've set them down.

Brief, echoing—which is to say great—short shorts have been emerging from the continually changing nucleus of writers around Pamela Painter's workshops at Emerson College for years now. In fact, each of these pieces has already been published in journals and books ranging from *Quick Fiction* to *StoryQuarterly* to *The Best American Non-Required Reading*, and it seemed to us high time to collect them. We are pleased to be able to do so in this, the first book from Rose Metal Press.

The empty space that short shorts have filled wasn't readily visible prior to their emergence, but now it's difficult to imagine the literary world without them. We hope that our press will come to fill a similar space.

In the future, Rose Metal Press hopes to continue to draw attention to, and provide a publishing forum for, exciting, frequently overlooked, and often under-represented hybrid genres. As we kick off that mission with *Brevity & Echo*, we express our deep and sincere gratitude for the support of Pamela Painter and Ron Carlson, as well as to the talented writers who've allowed us to include their wonderful work on these pages.

The longest story in *Brevity & Echo* weighs in at 1,400 words, the shortest at 55. Each of them requires only a small amount of time to read, but an uncertain amount of time to be done reading. They pull the reader back in and back in, because they are brief, because they echo.

In other words, we chose these pieces for their ability to encourage you to:

READ SHORT,
THINK LONG.

Enjoy.

Abigail Beckel
Kathleen Rooney
November 2006

INTRODUCTION: THE RIDE

RON CARLSON

Somewhere in your heart when you climb into a car on the roller coaster there is a small knowledge that in two minutes you will return to this weird little station with your hair messed up and two screams and a heartbeat short. When you step into a short short fiction, you can let go of that idea. You may get no further than the fact that the safety bar seems to be made out of sugar or that the ride operator looks a lot like your junior high science teacher and then as the gears engage, echoing like the coins tumbling out of a torn bag onto the marble floors of the Supreme Court and the vehicle grinds out and up into the sunlight where there is a train coming the other way, an important —if brief—dilemma, and always the thirteen sudden sidetracks with destination signs in the Cyrillic alphabet, none offering sleeper cars. There is a chance that the entire trip will be absolutely uphill until the oxygen masks drop from somewhere, precluding the opportunity to scream with any real efficacy. Then it's dark and all along the way music, voices chanting as if around a ceremonial fire, and the smell of fabric softener, and the bliss of knowing your fabrics are all soft enough, even in this wind which is now cold, and how long has it been winter? The short short fiction in *Brevity & Echo* sweeps us out into a sudden place and we should just go. Take a good look at the operator as you climb in; you won't see her again. You can hold on, but you're not coming back here.

Brevity & Echo

THE CUSTODIAN

BRIAN HINSHAW

The job would get boring if you didn't mix it up a little. Like this woman in 14-A, the nurses called her the mockingbird, start any song and this old lady would sing it through. Couldn't speak, couldn't eat a lick of solid food, but she sang like a house on fire. So for a kick, I would go in there with my mop and such, prop the door open with the bucket, and set her going. She was best at the songs you'd sing with a group—"Oh! Susanna," campfire stuff. Any kind of Christmas song worked good too, and it always cracked the nurses if I could get her into "Let It Snow" during a heat spell. We'd try to make her to take up a song from the radio or some of the old songs with cursing in them, but she would never go for those. Although once I had her do "How Dry I Am" while Nurse Winchell fussed with the catheter.

Yesterday, her daughter or maybe granddaughter comes in while 14-A and I were partways into "Auld Lang Syne" and the daughter says "oh oh oh" like she had interrupted scintillating conversation and then she takes a long look at 14-A lying there in the gurney with her eyes shut and her curled-up hands, taking a cup of kindness yet. And the daughter looks at me the way a girl does at the end of a old movie and she says "my god," says, "you're an angel," and now I can't do it anymore, can hardly step into her room.

Happy Families Are All the Same

CHIP CHEEK

Happy families are all alike; every unhappy family is unhappy in its own way. Happy families all share similar features; every unhappy family, however, is alien to every other, at least in terms of its unhappiness. Given any set of happy families, Family X will always be equal to Family Y, whereas in any given set of unhappy families, the unhappiness of any two families will never be equal. Happy families tend toward increasing homogeneity, while unhappy families, via the irrational ordering presence of the human mind, reverse this trend by giving rise to distinct, isolated systems of unhappiness. Though widespread variations exist among cultures and across time, stable and cohesive—that is to say, happy—families exhibit similar forms and behaviors within any given society (the nature of these forms and behaviors depending on the organization of the society in question, such as, for example, the patriarchal and class-based structure of wealthy Nineteenth Century Russian households), while fractured, inconstant—or, to put it simply, unhappy—families exhibit their unhappiness in widely diverse and mutually inimitable forms and behaviors (this diversity owing itself to the family members' irrational deviations from the norms of the society in question—for example, throwing oneself under the wheels of a passing railroad car). Happy families are all the same, but the Oblonsky family, with which this great novel you are presently reading begins, stands apart, distinct and individual, because it is unhappy. If it weren't for unhappiness, all families would be the same. Thankfully, not all families are happy, because happy families are all identical and that would make an exceedingly monotonous book—and, as you will see, the families in this book are refreshingly dissimilar. The Oblonsky family is not like other families: the Oblonsky family is very unhappy (but in a way that is different from other unhappy families). Happy families are all alike, which may comfort some people and bore others, but whatever one's feelings about happy families, surely everyone can agree that, at the very least, each and every unhappy family offers a new and exciting experience of unhappiness, which surely must be worth something, at least for great novels like this one, which will include such unhappy distinctions as deceptive French governesses; drunken siblings who date prostitutes; cuckolded Russian aristocrats who attempt to mask their philistinism with an interest in Beethoven; full-grown women named Kitty; stuffy, itchy, red-velvety dinner parties and balls; and, of course, innovative methods of suicide. Happiness in families is always general and abstract, while unhappiness is specific and concrete. Unhappy families bear no precedents and yet they are everywhere, while happy families seem to copy themselves over and over again and at the same time exist in no tangible place, the reason for this being clear on closer inspection, namely, that there are really no such things as happy families.

Nebraska

ASHLEY RICE

Rebecca Morgan's wings appeared on the same crisp day her mother left on a Greyhound for Las Vegas to the land of salvation, quick change and slot machines, where (her mother wrote in her goodbye letter) everything was or where everything was that mattered, and where anything that seemed to matter even halfway could easily be put into a slogan.

When Rebecca woke up in her four-square plywood room aware of an empty feel to the house she had grown up in, there they were, and the huge, ridiculous wings would follow her through physical education and health classes in the Hawthorne-like sawmill town she lived in. The woods her step-father roamed as a child still echoed with shotgun blasts, freezing winters, vacancy, or death, and under coal-blackened, cold skies she somehow dreamed of being a starlet.

In a red school nestled in trees beneath billboards and in an abandoned glass factory's bottle-neck shaped shadow, she hid these new wings under clothes.

"Like we can't see them—ho *ha*," from Kenny Blackburn, a boy she'd had a hard, slow crush on since forever. He leaned against his locker, laughed, glanced back at Rebecca as she walked away, and leaned back again, red-faced.

The wings were bird-useless (could not fly), but as far as Rebecca was concerned, they never gave her any trouble until her senior year of high school. When she won the chocolate-selling contest and saw a counselor about community college she did not yet know that her own life and her step-father's small house would soon turn into a vacant lot. Hoping to match their lives fashion-wise to snazzy billboards and magazine ads, no one at school would talk to her. Fashion was impossible. Jean jackets were cut too small through the back, so Rebecca Morgan would pull sweatshirts on over her wings. During finals, the chore of hiding the large white feathers took *so* long, though, so she simply cut awkward holes in the back of navy sweaters and forgot about them.

Then Kenny was killed in a mill accident.

A semi-truck carrying dark chocolate and oranges hit black ice, slipped over the ridge and crashed through, destroying treetops, then plummeted.

The two events weren't related or in any way portentous, but for many people felt like an omen, the same way her father's house being cut down like a tree for a shopping center felt like one. The trees were changing and the world was rearranging itself, maybe—somewhat, somehow—or perhaps not really. The kids in town made Rebecca into a winged mascot then. They didn't say anything when they put gold glitter on her thin arms, and she didn't say anything or push away when they wanted to dance in a circle around her, or unfold her wings like origami at parties.

There was a one-sentence story engraved on a local bar's wall that said "Crows in the snow, and the moon doesn't know." It had been crossed out years ago with a sharp welding tool, and people remembered it as meaning "Do whatever you want," but Rebecca Morgan interpreted this as "Do whatever you can." She liked the saying and she felt very powerful thinking about it.

One night she saw her silhouette across the faded grass and thought she also saw her mother, years before: tall and white-winged and all ready to go—dancing yet somehow static—like the doctored sign at the end of the oak-colored road, which said: *You are now leaving Nebraska.* Though they did not live in Nebraska.

Tulip

CHRISTOPHER HELMUTH

From the beginning I am all out in opposition against the purchase of the dog Irving because I know he will die and I have had too much of the dogs dying in my life already to this point. The dog Lucas drown in a pool. The dog Shadow stung in his ear with a bee. The dog Tiger crushed in a crumpled Corolla. On and on, always me with the crying and the empty rhinestone collar and the dog missing out of it. I am saying no way is my baby having that. I am saying no way my tulip will be knowing all the pain from the constant dying of dogs.

But of course the dog Irving is cute and small and lonely seeming and I buy him not listening to the sense of me but to the please please please of my baby with her mama's eyes and sure enough a year later much M&M candy is fed the dog Irving and he dies.

So days are passing and there I am again, broken, thinking why must this always be, but also knowing for sure it is long past time to be talking to my tulip regarding the ending state of things. I go over to where she is viewing the cartoons and I say let's us two go outside for a while and we do. We are here sitting on the grainy concrete of the steps and I am taking the golden hair of my baby in these fingers of mine and wondering what do I say of all that is awful and true. I am thinking, she will cry. I am thinking, she will ask for another and he will also die. I am thinking, she will come to me and I will hold her close and I will let no other living things come close by.

Before I am bringing myself to speak, my baby, she slips from my arms. She hops from life to life, from inchworm to ladybug to butterfly. There she is now, in her yellow dress, kneeling on the sidewalk. Look at her. My tulip. Smiling her mama's crinkled smile. Lopping the heads off all the ants with her tiny pink thumbnails.

Love and Other Catastrophes: A Mix Tape

AMANDA HOLZER

"All By Myself" (Eric Carmen). "Looking for Love" (Lou Reed). "I Wanna Dance With Somebody" (Whitney Houston). "Let's Dance" (David Bowie). "Let's Kiss" (Beat Happening). "Let's Talk About Sex" (Salt N' Pepa). "Like A Virgin" (Madonna). "We've Only Just Begun" (The Carpenters). "I Wanna Be Your Boyfriend" (The Ramones). " I'll Tumble 4 Ya" (Culture Club). "Head Over Heels" (The Go-Go's). "Nothing Compares To You" (Sinéad O'Connor). "My Girl" (The Temptations). "Could This Be Love" (Bob Marley). "Love and Marriage" (Frank Sinatra). "White Wedding" (Billy Idol). "Stuck in the Middle with You" (Steelers Wheel). "Tempted" (Squeeze). "There Goes My Baby" (The Drifters). "What's Going On" (Marvin Gaye). "Where Did You Sleep Last Night" (Leadbelly). "Whose Bed Have Your Boots Been Under?" (Shania Twain). "Jealous Guy" (John Lennon). "Your Cheatin' Heart" (Tammy Wynette). "Shot Through the Heart" (Bon Jovi). "Don't Go Breaking My Heart" (Elton John and Kiki Dee). "My Achy Breaky Heart" (Billy Ray Cyrus). "Heartbreak Hotel" (Elvis Presley). "Stop, In the Name of Love" (The Supremes). "Try a Little Tenderness" (Otis Redding). "Try (Just a Little Bit Harder)" (Janis Joplin). "All Apologies" (Nirvana). "Hanging on the Telephone" (Blondie). "I Just Called to Say I Love You" (Stevie Wonder). "Love Will Keep Us Together" (Captain and Tennille). "Let's Stay Together" (Al Green). "It Ain't Over 'Til It's Over" (Lenny Kravitz). "What's Love Got To Do With It?" (Tina Turner). "You Don't Bring Me Flowers Anymore" (Barbara Streisand and Neil Diamond). "I Wish You

Wouldn't Say That" (Talking Heads). "You're So Vain" (Carly Simon). "Love Is a Battlefield" (Pat Benatar). "Heaven Knows I'm Miserable Now" (The Smiths). "(Can't Get No) Satisfaction" (The Rolling Stones). "Must Have Been Love (But It's Over Now)" (Roxette). "Breaking Up Is Hard to Do" (Neil Sedaka). "I Will Survive" (Gloria Gaynor). "Hit the Road, Jack" (Mary McCaslin and Jim Ringer). "These Boots Were Made for Walking" (Nancy Sinatra). "All Out of Love" (Air Supply). "All By Myself" (Eric Carmen).

The History You've Been Trying to Write

JOANNE AVALLON

Your arm and hand cock back instinctively, although they have never moved like this before, because your first-born has taken a piece of your thigh between her two-year-old, sharp and white incisors, and it surprises you to find your arm in this position, you who dress her naked dolls so they won't look cold, but her teeth take deeper hold and drive everything out of your head except, oddly, your own father saying "silly bitch" when you were five and left your bike out in the rain and also the sound, so compelling, of skin hitting skin and, even more oddly, something your aunt told you about your grandfather boxing your father's ear so bad it bled rough red stuff from the eardrum—all this, even the love you feel for both these men, rushes through you so fast you understand for the first time—as your hand descends—the phrase "seeing red" and the only thing between your hand and your child is your puny intellect scared shitless in some corner, so that just before your hand hits the tender part of her thigh, the part you had kissed just twenty minutes ago when changing her diaper and before she screams, your daughter looks at you first in disbelief and then in complete comprehension, as though, perhaps she knew these stories all along, and you wonder, with terror, like you've never wondered before, if this is the history you've been trying to write.

Games My Father Played

DERRICK ABLEMAN

Peek-a-Boo
An early favorite of ours. My father vanished behind his hands with consummate grace and skill, staying gone long enough to achieve the right amount of suspense. Later, his talents here would dull, forcing him to resort to all manner of prop and pyrotechnic: blindfolding me with a blanket, crouching behind furniture, spinning my chair. But always his hands were evident in the act; you could hear him knock things over on his way to obscurity, stumbling into the doorframe, stubbing his toe and cursing to reveal himself.

Basketball
We had a hoop in the driveway one summer, a real one, regulation height and everything. The neighbor kids, who were older, taller, and knew how to play, would come over and hog it. They brought their own balls and held court while my parents were away at work. One time my Dad was home while they were harassing me some—throwing for the head, fouling me hard, stuff like that. He watched for a while from the kitchen window, then took his car out of the garage and parked under the hoop. He climbed on the hood and hung from the rim until it gave and lost shape.

Croquet
I played this with my cousin once, in somebody's yard, during a family reunion. My father set up the rings, laid out the rules and returned to the grill, beer in hand, sandals clicking through the

thick grass. But we quit early; the lanes were hard to keep straight and the mallets were begging for misuse. Besides, the game was sissy and hard and we'd had enough fooling around. We wanted to do something serious. We were found sometime later, at the edge of a deep woods, smashing full beers with our toy hammers, stinking to high heaven.

Catch

Catch is not baseball. It's better. It's catch. Stand as far away as possible, until you can't see the other person's eyes, until their face becomes unclear. Keep quiet. Now, between you there is the ball, sailing back and forth, easy as you please. It makes a sound when it meets the mitt, when it's caught. It makes another sound when it's traveling through the air, just before it's caught. Strung together, these sounds are like talking.

Tag

Ruthless. He never once checked his adult abilities in the spirit of fair play; pursuing at top speeds, pushing when necessary, always willing to hook you by the collar and drag back a few grassy yards before slapping your belly, cursing you "it."

The same was true of the reverse direction; he fled faster than he chased, putting his heart all the way into it, sometimes going blocks and blocks beyond the yard and staying gone for the rest of the day. Once you were "it" with my father, the condition was permanent.

Monopoly

Here I got a taste for blood. I was master of the board—patient with my properties, careful with my fortunes. My father showed no restraint, no sense of planning, and so would avoid the purchase of any space that wasn't "strictly Boardwalk." Meanwhile I snapped up the less appealing parts of town, built up homes, then hotels. I launched my empire from the ghetto while my father squandered his turns on financing scraps of easy street. I loaned him money to cover his rents. I fronted him capital for his real house. "It's an investment," he'd say. "Not a loan. In time, we'll be penthouse partners." My head swam with foreclosures and seized properties.

Spotlight
A night game. Camping in the North Woods. We borrowed a pickup truck and tent from my uncle. The flashlight was mine. The idea, my father's. He sat in the flatbed of the truck on a lawn chair, drinking a beer and waving the flashlight into the woods. I would be hiding in the woods, stalking toward him, avoiding the light and moving without a sound. If I touched the truck without getting caught, I won.

"Win what?" I asked.

"You'll see," he said.

Hide and Go Seek
These are agreed upon absences, tiny contracts of vanishing between us. I close my eyes and count in years. I count in zip codes. He moves out of town, apartment to apartment. I move too. Phones change and postcards drift through my mailbox. Jonesburg. Dallas. Portland. Saint Paul. I put these on the wall as I get them. They are dated and this, I think, is his way of leaving a trail, his form of breadcrumb. They're all frauds. You can see it in his signature, can tell it by his hand, the way his name creeps off the bottom of the card, as though done in invisible ink.

Party Favors

NINA R. SCHNEIDER

The mother is a mental health professional who, during post-partum delirium, named her daughter Psyche, and now it's time for Psyche's bat mitzvah, which is in search of a theme, but not with the usual cutesy party favors and blue, white, and silver balloon arches of her friends. . . . Psyche chooses to be socially conscious, she announced in the Rabbi's study, as he perused her speech condemning the over-prescribing of Ritalin to children, she—thirteen years old going on thirty—wants to use this God-given opportunity, her bat mitzvah party, to "educate" family and friends about mental illness, even though it stumps the party planner, an expert on themes featuring glitter-encrusted Styrofoam ballerinas, pivoting hockey players, or Mylar-leafed palm trees as centerpieces, and sits speechless as Psyche advocates for the only theme she likes—a "Psyche-o-rama" as she describes it from her dream the previous evening: decorate each adult table with linens in shades of gray, a unique sign and party favors: Bi-polar illness (key-chain masks for comedy/tragedy); Depression (sad-faced ceramic clowns), Phobias (decks of cards with photos of dogs, elevators and bridges), and Schizophrenia (audio-cassettes), while the kids' tables might feature Attention Deficit Disorder (ping-pong balls), ADD with Hyperactivity (ping pong balls and slinkies), and Anorexia Nervosa (empty plates). Her anxiety-ridden mother asks Psyche where they could possibly seat her father, who's just filed for divorce but won't move out until after the celebration. Psyche, insightful beyond her years, declares,

"There will be no sign at Dad's table—it's the one for Denial (happy face lollipops)."

Diverging Paths and All That

MARYANNE O'HARA

In Dollar Saver, the aisles are empty, customers crowding Electronics watching Nixon resign on twenty TV sets. Dad dropped us off with three bucks to buy burgers, but we've already spent it on fireballs and fudge.

While Nixon keeps the manager occupied, Billy demonstrates the "heads-up technique," the nonchalant gaze, his left hand filching Hershey bars and Bic pens while his right hand jingles pocket change. Billy grins, "I really save my dollars here."

Solo time. I head for Cosmetics, the wall of Peeper Sticks—blue and green and lavender eye crayons that've always cost dollars I don't have. My hand closes around Seafoam Green, hesitates, but what the hell, even the President's a crook, so I slip it up my sleeve. I try to sneak away natural as Billy, but my legs move too quick and stiff.

Billy meets me in Electronics, where Nixon's keeping his head up, not admitting a damn thing. Saying he'd be able to clear his name if he fought long enough, but he'll sacrifice his honor for the country. When he says he'll resign as of noon the next day, I check out all these adults who yelled, "Impeach the crook." Nobody cheers. The faces are solemn as gravestones. Billy's motioning, Come on let's go, but I suddenly feel like I ate too much candy. I shake my sleeve, dropping the Peeper Stick onto a shelf, and follow Billy out the automatic doors. Dad's picking us up in two minutes, but Billy's headed someplace else.

How To Make Potato Salad

STEVE HIMMER

1. Decide to make potato salad.

2. Boil 8–10 red potatoes and 6 eggs in heavily salted water. Remember that the first chef you worked under taught you to salt egg-boiling water because the salt breaks down membranes between shell and meat, making the egg easier to peel later on. Decide that was the best job you've ever had.

3. While eggs and potatoes boil, think about doing some writing. Decide to make Rice Krispie squares instead. Remember that the restaurant was named after a character in a novel you've never read, and that she was a prostitute. Laugh about that. Decide to read the novel, and mean it this time. Remember mixing potato salad in plastic garbage pails, with your arms up to the elbows in mayonnaise and balsamic vinegar. Realize you'd never heard of balsamic vinegar before learning to make potato salad according to your first chef's recipe.

4. Dice half of a red onion and sautée it in olive oil. Add 4 cloves of minced garlic. Note that cooking the onions is not part of chef's recipe, but do it anyway. While getting garlic from the refrigerator, notice most of a six-pack. Wonder if it's too early to start drinking yet. Imagine what Miss Manners would say:

Dear Miss Manners,
At what time is it appropriate for one to open the first beer of the day?
Signed, Thirsty

Dear Thirsty,
There's no single specific time that is appropriate, and there are certain times of the year at which drinking earlier is more acceptable. But if you find yourself struggling to resist the "first beer of the day," you might consider trying to not drink it at all. Alcohol should be an occasional. . .wait, what are. . .you couldn't even wait until I finished answering? How crass!

Decide that Ms. Manners is a fuddy duddy. Wonder if you've ever called anyone a "fuddy duddy" before, and if that means you're becoming one, too.

5. Remove potatoes and eggs from heat. Drain and leave in the sink to cool. Open the first beer of the day. Give Miss Manners the finger, wherever she is.

6. Add 3 smoked sausages (thinly sliced) to the onions and garlic over medium heat, tossing the pan occasionally. Think about the first time you had potato salad with sausage in it, in Germany. Remember how nice Stüttgart was at Christmas, and how long it's been since you spoke to your friends there. Think about other friends you fell out of touch with, and wonder how you might reach them. Wonder, too, if you ever ate potato salad in Finland while visiting other friends you haven't talked to in years. Try to remember how long it's been since the restaurant you first worked in went out of business, and what all the other people who worked there are doing now.

7. Remove onions, garlic, and sausages from heat. Decide that if you ever open a restaurant, you will also name it after a hooker. Forget that the pan is still hot and pick it up without a sidetowel. Blister.

8. Chop the potatoes and put them in a big bowl. Open the second beer of the day. Think that Miss Manners may know more

than you gave her credit for, but also think that a cold bottle brings welcome relief to burnt fingers.

9. Peel the eggs using the palm-rolling motion chef taught you when you were 14. Remember when you wanted to be a chef. Decide that yes, maybe you would like to open a restaurant someday.. Roughly chop the eggs and add them to the bowl, then add the cooled onion, garlic, and sausage.

10. Add a dollop of mayonnaise to the bowl. Wonder who came up with the word "dollop." Add a spoonful of Dijon mustard and a few shakes of balsamic vinegar. Add a bit more balsamic vinegar. Mix it all up using the mahogany spoon you carved when you moved to Maine because you wanted to build wooden boats for a living. Try to remember how many things you've wanted to do for a living. Wonder what you're going to do for a living.

11. S & P tt. Laugh about how much you've always enjoyed the rhyme of "S & P tt." Remember how many things were funny at your first job, in the restaurant named after a prostitute. Remember Herb & Onion bread, and the superhero you invented named Urban Onion, and remember that you never thought of any powers for Urban Onion to have, only a name. Remember how saying "86 the clam chowder" felt so precise, like you were a surgeon, and that working as an observer of heart surgeries performed by famous doctors wasn't half as much fun as making potato salad in a restaurant named for a woman who didn't really exist.

12. Sit on the couch watching Food TV with an enormous bowl of potato salad beside you. Open the third beer of the day. Remember when you opened the first.

Gory Joy

JOE ROBB

That Jimmy had AB-blood became apparent only after injury, when he'd pull his blood-donor card from his wallet and fidget. It was a habit learned from his father, a hemophiliac who nervously fingered his blood-type card at the first sign of bruising. Though Jimmy was not a hemophiliac, he was a klutz and pulled out his card nearly as often as his father. From day one he was clumsy, seemingly unable to avoid pricks, punctures, slashes or stabs. A pick slipped. Slate shingles fell, twirling end over keen-edged end. A loose, jolted trailer hitch lurched down to the asphalt, unable to deny gravity its due. Couldn't help that Jimmy's foot was in the way. Hell, even the doctor couldn't reattach the toe Jimmy left in the driveway that day because the trailer was too heavy to lift without steroids or hydraulics and Jimmy believed in neither. And, when questioned, the endless parade of bent fork tines swear they meant to grab, not to slip and jab.

"There's just so much pressure," they say. "What would you do if someone was grinding your head into porcelain? Something's got to give, and plate faces are known for their hard-nosedness. The path of least resistance tends to rip plumb through the web of skin between Jimmy's thumb and forefinger. It just tears so nicely."

But the superlative receptivity of Jimmy's blood type came to light only after the really big accidents—falling out of hot air balloons and such. Then came the familiar drone of the ambulance siren, the snug embrace of stretcher straps straining against the torso, the almost lecherous winks of the EMTs.

They'd flip on the blood box, pop the cooler lid, and pull out a bag at random. Sometimes they'd even giggle and close their eyes. Needle-pierce vein, pop bag, jiggle IV, repeat until full. No worries. Jimmy was too big to die, too large for himself, a moiling panoply of variegated blood cells, natives stiffly nodding to foreigners at the behest of those already naturalized. Jim's capillaries housed no riots, rebellions, or renegades. No racism or religious squabbles. No rough stuff allowed; inequality forbidden. A rosy utopia pumped through Jim's veins, giving him a ruddy glow that was often mistaken for enlightenment. Don't it make you wish for more Jimmies?

CASINO

DENISE DUHAMEL

When my sister says *there's been an accident*, I think *car*, then *bus*, but she says no "escalator" and "pile-up" and I picture the bodies, my mother on the bottom of fifteen casino-goers, her hair (a perm) caught in the moving steps—bump bump bump—against her back. Someone pulls the bodies off one by one and lifts my mother as though she is light as a dust mote. A man sits her on the dirty casino carpet, the top of my mother's head pulled away. Someone else puts my mother's purse in her lap, and my father, fifth in the pile-up, finally finds my mother, sees her sitting there, like a shocked little girl. He tries to walk towards her, her bloody face, but faints, then crawls to her instead. My mother's eyes are as blank as tokens.

When my sister says the word "scalped," I think cowboys and Indians, tiny shrunken heads, the blood all boiled out, warpaths.

Yellow chips polka dot around my parents and the other people who've fallen on the escalator. Coupons for complimentary lunches. A few desperate passers-by pick up the free money instead of helping, quarters streaked with blood darkening their days.

My father curls like a cashew around my mother so she can lean into him. Workers circle both of my parents, to shield them from the stares of tourists out for a drink and a game of slots. My father's left hand is all cut up, his wedding band is shredded and sharp. He doesn't know yet about his heart, how he'll be hooked up to the monitors soon.

I remember my mother telling me to braid my hair before riding the Ferris wheel and a story about a girl's loose curls flying into the gears, being torn out in chunks, her blood, warm red specks, dripping onto the seats below. And how the carnie had to stop the ride with a jolt and how a fireman shot up in a bucket truck with a pair of scissors to release the screaming girl. When the ride went back on, the passengers got off, one by one, no one smiling or laughing any more. And I was never sure if my mother was on that ride or in the park that day or if it was just a story she liked to tell. The girl's hair scattered, whipping by the horses in the Merry-Go-Round, twisting into the cotton candy.

And my mother's hair, also left behind in some gear, her blood soaking the silver escalator steps, the casino carpet.

Up and down and round and round. All the bald lemons and cherries spinning.

Baldness

MARK DECARTERET

The toupee he found at a prizefight on the counter of a souvenir stand smelled of pickled eggs and Christmas colognes. Though he had plenty of hair he liked the way it sat on his head like a cargo of wisecracks. Hugging him, one of his hands would be strumming my back while the other adjusted the piece. Always wary of his cigar and its alien eye, I would soak up his buttery warmth, any thoughts about his toupee resembling the scalp of a joke store gorilla sliding down my whole body to rest in my toes. He went weeks without washing his own hair, forcing my aunt to insist he sleep in the den. That's when he started taking drinks, stopped showing up for his job at the shoe factory. Not just drinking to smother a streak of bad luck or help a neighbor celebrate twins. This was different. This was a tunnel leading out into space. A tunnel black and greedy like the throat of a snake. Day and night he could be found on the couch, reaching behind the throw pillow heavy with sweat from his head. Years later when they found him in the cellar, hanging from an overhead pipe, the first thing I noticed was his hairlessness. The pinkest of globes like an unforeseen witness, its radiance attempting to capture our surprise. In this corner long-surrendered to spiders and the husks of flying things, we discovered the bottles set up in rows like a carnival game. My aunt said the smell of spent liquor made her ill, but to a boy of my age it only suggested miles of river foam, monstrous gears mashing bone into invisible stars. Out the bulkhead they carried his body, his stomach even more spectacular beneath the white sheet. And when the poorest variety of daylight snuck in, I noticed the toupees, hanging from nails above his workbench. The one he'd found at the prizefight and the one we presumed to be his own hair, as well as many others, all colors and styles, of which I couldn't tell you a thing.

Funny Things That Happen

MATT RITTENHOUSE

Many rich women, especially in New York, had bracelets of bees flying twisting circles around their wrists and necks. These women thought it gave them a natural, carefree presence, when at parties they would take the bees off, and drape them on the flowers in vases. Throughout the party the bees would buzz about the flowers, forgetting what to do with their fuzzy legs and the pollen.

When it was time to go, the women would, while laughing and finishing their drinks, extend their hands into the blooms, and the bees would stop circling the roses or whatever, and start circling the delicate wrists outstretched. The ladies could then leave, knowing they had brought a little of the way things once were with them.

Fancy Footwork

R. S. STEINBERG

A rebel barricade stopped their tour bus in the mountains. The masked leader shot the driver who tried to radio; they let Amy keep her iPod.

Hands-free, Steven dialed her father at the embassy.

The leader brandished his machine gun. *"¿Teléfono?"*

"¡Música!" Steven yelped, and kept dancing that crazy step until Mr. Wilcox answered.

Star Light

SHANNON HUFFMAN

That October, pumpkin carving time, we pick up a perfectly round ten-pounder at the farm down the road. Cut triangle eyes, a slit nose, and a toothy grin that looks like my husband's when he's told a bad joke. We officially name the jack o' lantern Mephistopheles because of this evil grin, but we call him Jack because it's easier to pronounce. During the day Jack looks out the front window of our condo; at night we move him to the kitchen table where we can see him. We didn't go through all the work of creating him not to see him. At dinner, we pretend to feed Jack. My husband stuffs a piece of bread between Jack's teeth and says, *Don't forget to chew*. Then we say Jack's favorite food is macaroni and cheese. His favorite color is green. His favorite word is kitty. We say that he doesn't like carrots, but will eat them if he's promised dessert. That he's most ticklish on the back of his neck. That when he sings, he sounds like a warbly record, and when he cries he sounds like cats fighting. We say that in Little League he will hit the game-winning run. That in the fourth grade spelling bee he will successfully spell *rhythm*, *endeavor,* and *situation*, but that he will lose to a girl who spells *discomfiture*. That the first CD he will buy without us knowing will be Green Day. We say that in high school, he will get his girlfriend pregnant. That in college, he will cheat on his finals. That on his first job, he will get fired for stealing paper clips. We know these things about Jack as if he were our own, as if we had our own.

Planned road trip to South Carolina a week later, we belt Jack into the back seat. He's pretty quiet, pretty well behaved, we say.

In Pennsylvania, we pick up I81 and watch the road open up and lead us through rolling pasture. And as the sun sets over the land and the first hint of darkness comes, we say, *Star light, star bright, first star I see tonight*. We make our wishes, no matter how fanciful they are. In the morning though, Jack has gotten bad. Slippery lips, looking kind of green. My husband tries to scrape the mold off Jack with a pocket knife, but when he does, Jack's teeth fall out. The next to go is his nose. And soon he's nothing more than a caved-in mess that has leaked onto three towels and a motel bedspread. *It's time*, we say. So we put him in the middle of the field behind the Super 8. For a few seconds we stare at the cell phone tower that marks where we've left Jack. Then we turn to each other. *For the best*, we say. *For the best*. Then we get in the car and go because our baby is gone.

MELON

LESLIE BUSLER

At a fruit stand off the old farm-to-market near Magnolia, I picked out a watermelon that had been shot by vandals. While painting a sign—Bludgeoned Fruit, 75% off—the owner told us much of the produce had sustained mere flesh wounds at the hands of the hoodlums, but this watermelon suffered a good blow to the gut, and looking at it, I couldn't help but feel punctured myself.

Marla had said, "Can't we get a normal one?" Looking pale and shapeless amid the carnage, she took an emery board from her purse and began to file her fingernails over a flat of strawberries. I placed my palm on the melon's wound as she covered the whiskered berries with a light dusting, then brushed the remaining powder onto a pile of plums.

Caressing the melon, I said, "Have a heart, Marla. Can't you?"

I took the watermelon home, set it on the front porch, and waited for a revelation. When one didn't come Marla grew irritated and a bit homicidal. One day she went inside and returned with the electric steak knife and a fat, squat wooden saltshaker.

"Marla," I said, "hasn't there been enough violence?"

The watermelon sat untouched near a pot of geraniums until the bottom rotted, the bullet hole puckered, and things came to live inside it. Marla urged its disposal, but I liked to watch the levels of decay, liked its morbid, gangly presence. I was that ant or inchworm, that fat, prickly caterpillar burrowing nooks with high vaulted ceilings, dozing in a patch of sun breaking through the bulleted skylight.

One evening Marla said, "The watermelon has caved in completely." So with a snow shovel from the hall closet I scooped the decomposed parts from the porch and carried them around to the backyard, where I scattered the remains over the compost heap. From the kitchen window Marla watched. I imagined her mouthing something. *I love you*? Unlikely. *You don't bring me flowers any*—Probably not. *There lies the last of our ancient past, decomposed and lifeless*. Well it's nice to think so. And I mouthed, *But the seeds, Marla. The seeds*.

Leaning toward the window, Marla pressed her lips against the wire mesh. She opened her mouth, hesitated. Before she backed away from the screen I thought I saw her brush her cheek with the tips of her fingers, and the gesture caught my heart a little.

I slipped my hands into my pockets and began steady, measured steps toward the house. There were twenty-three logs in a stack near the patio (I counted); there was a stone on the doormat (I kicked it). At the screen door I paused, then stepped into the shadowy kitchen. Marla stood quiet for a minute, then she said, "Are you finished now? Are you done with all of that?"

Buttermelon

BRAIIAN RUUSKA

The entire time I was there I tried to avoid my grandmother's kitchen, but as her lungs filled with the black fluid she became increasingly insistent that I get her a glass of water.

Her kitchen looked much the same as it did the last time I'd been there, as a child. It was quite ordinary: table, chairs, cupboards, refrigerator. What repulsed me was none of these things, but what she used to feed me at that table each summer. It was watermelon, which usually would have been considered quite a treat in this part of town; indeed, the watermelon truck hadn't visited our neighborhood in years.

But the watermelon my grandmother bought didn't taste like it came from a truck, or even this earth; it tasted like butter. Based on what I'd learned about the making of butter (you churn it) and the making of watermelon (you plant seeds), I could never comprehend how this might have been possible. And as my grandmother lay there on her deathbed, all I wanted was to ask her where it came from. Did she put watermelon seeds in a churn, churn them vigorously, then bury the churn for several weeks until the seeds had grown? That was the only explanation I could come up with, even after all these years.

I realized I must have been yelling "How?" repeatedly when I heard my grandmother's voice rise up through those black fluid-filled lungs, informing me that the glasses were in the middle cupboard.

How To Be a Real Ballerina

Jane Berentson

Grow out your hair. Grow out your bangs. Quit math team. Quit soccer. Quit wearing underwear. Learn words like *solar plexus* and *momentum*. Use them on the playground. Find heroes with Eastern European names. Learn French phrases like *pas de chat*. Think of them as names of steps—not as another language. Spend afternoons on wood floors. Don't grip the bar too tight. Cut holes in the feet of your tights so you can tend to your toes. Tape your toes. Don't pop blisters. Slather your feet in Preparation H. Don't be embarrassed to buy Preparation H. Wear a tampon the very first time. Keep lavender in your shoe bag. Keep your toe nails trim. Stay trim. Drink Diet Pepsi. Eat rice cakes. Pretend you like rice cakes. Learn that *pas de chat* means "step like a cat." Let your *pas de chats* improve. Abstain from growing breasts. Stretch every day. Tell guys how flexible you are. Talk shit. Talk shit about the snow queen's *fouté* turns. Point your toes while watching television. Turn out your hips while sitting in a desk. Ignore college brochures, college fairs, career counselors, your parents. Get an apartment with a clothesline so your tights and leotards can dance in the wind without you. Stay mysterious. Wear scarves year round and sandals imported from exotic locations. Smoke, but keep bobby pins in the ashtray of your car. Try heroin once. Pose for the mug shot of your resumé. Tilt your head while thinking *mature grace* and *classic elegance*. Get a part time job at an art museum. Count everything in eights, but waltzes in threes. Suck in. Turn out. Pull up. Lower your shoulders. Relax your wrists. Now smile. Smile at the pianist. Flirt with the pianist. Sleep with the pianist, but caress your prince's cheek like you love him. Cuss when he nearly drops you. Notice the bruises on your ribs. Wax all your pubic hair. Use aerosol hairspray, but eat organic fruit. Drink black coffee, but whiten your teeth. Use body glitter sparingly. Dance the role of a swan, but sometimes forget to think of your arms as wings. Lengthen your neck. At the 24-hour diner, wipe your lipstick on your napkin and peel off your fake eyelashes. While the pianist is in the bathroom, sneak the lashes next to his omelet. Arrange them to look like a spider. Say "I know" when he says you were beautiful. Laugh when he gasps at his plate. Hoist your cardigan around the shadowy lines of your collar bones. Now curtsy.

Girl Talk

LAURA VAN DEN BERG

"He could be a cad," my mother says, examining the wallet-sized photo of my lover. The diner is empty, the blinds partially closed; pale beams of sunlight hold particles of dust. I am facing the back door and the exit sign that hangs over it. The light inside the sign has burned out; the letters are dark and colorless. My mother cocks her head, and the red vinyl booth squeaks underneath her thighs. It is the middle of the day, and we are both drinking iced tea spiked with the rum she brought in a tin flask. She holds the photo in a stream of daylight and dust, as though the right lighting will uncover all the dark things behind his eyes. "Yes," she concludes. "He's bad all right. Run, that's my advice."

"I don't know that," I say, plucking the photo from her stubby fingertips and pressing it face down against the table. I wrap my lips around the straw and suck in a mouthful of tea and rum.

"Take my word for it." She fishes an ice cube out of the glass and rubs it all over her face and neck, polishes the gray pockets underneath her eyes. The diner is hot.

"But I'm young," I say. "It's my job to be optimistic."

She digs out another ice cube and slips it between her lips. "That's all fine," she says, sounding at once hollow and angry, crunching the ice with her teeth. "But you should know what to do in the event of an emergency."

Dear Mr. President

AMY L. CLARK

Dear Mr. President,

Right after you run your fingers, one at a time, through the hair directly above my ear, you start talking about Social Security, but I cannot forget the fact that you are 35 years older than me. Even in my dream I know that you are much more likely to benefit from all of the policies that you advocate than I am. Viagra, though wonderful for our relationship, will not mask the fact that I started working when I was 14 and still have no faith that I will retire before I die or the planet implodes.

I know that you wouldn't have gone gray if you didn't have such enormous daily responsibility. And yes, your power was what attracted me to you in the first place. But here's why I have to break it off: after September 11, I heard a lot of people your age compare the destruction to Pearl Harbor, to the explosion of American barracks in Africa, to what our bombers did in Yugoslavia, to Vietnam. I said: I am 21 years old. This does not remind me of anything. My hair turned gray anyway.

In my sex fantasy, while you and I are naked, my mouth covering your left nipple, I ask you for the last time: what is the opposite of death and destruction? Because I'm not sure, but I don't think that it is sex with you. Or anything with you. Not tonight. Not in my dream.

Sincerely,

Amy

Out of Africa

TARA L. MASIH

Yesterday I received your postcard from Africa. So innocuous, the tacky scrap of souvenir roared its warning—a pride of lions in cheap four-color processed photo inserts, profiled against savanna grass. (Lions not snarling look like gentle tabbies.) You write of wildlife, skies, lodgings, address me as "lady" and include me in the all-inclusive "we." But you are a dark magician, and your vanishing act—four seasons—was of the blackest order. The card's rounded creasing tells me that it was trapped in your back pocket before being mailed. And I wonder at your casualness, placing this oh-so-loaded message back there as thoughtlessly as you'd tuck away a comb, a wallet. To think you actually had to buy a stamp for this. Why? You want a reply. Why now?

Last night a spider the size of a man's fist crept up my bedcovers. I screamed and pulled on the overhead light chain, searched but couldn't find it. I'd thrown it off.

We Change Our Names

BETH ANNE ROYER

In the divine afterlife I pray there are spinach vendors. My husband will partake, having heard on the radio from a man who insists that raw spinach snacks saved his life. Dean is looking to re-invent himself through health, he has given up coffee and corn syrup, he has changed his name to Silas.

In his dreams, he is always stuck in a traffic jam near the Boston Garden trying to deliver some portion of a corpse to its next appointment. He wakes up and calls me Gloria; he wakes up and devours spinach. I wonder if these dreams are because he is studying electrons with the daughter of a funeral home director—or if they appear because it is January, the anniversary of his father's suicide—and the weather will not grant us a reprieve.

Even my grandfather, an ice cutter upstate, calls this a cold winter. I cook warm soups and sausage for supper. I answer when he says, "Gloria, where's the bread?" but I feel like a husk without my real name.

I drink sodas I hide in the toilet tank. I need to feel the shivery whisper of fizz in my throat. I drink sodas when Silas falls asleep on the carpet on dark afternoons. I watch the dogs outside playing vicious. When they are done, they drag their sodden bodies to the door.

They howl and I let them in, let them roll the ice off their bodies and onto the couch. They nuzzle Silas with their wet heads and he lies numb. "Silas," I call him, "Silas," and the storm windows shake in their casements, and the dogs sigh, and he does not wake up until I call him by his real name, Dean.

July

KIMBERLY ANN SOUTHWICK

When we get real bored, we ask Nipple (whose real name is Amanda, Sarah just started calling her Nipple one day because she heard it meant "idiot" in British slang), we ask her if we can smash the old television that her Mom's new boyfriend Tommy lugged to the curb earlier that day to make room for the new one they won off the radio, and she asks her Mom who says "sure," sipping a cheap beer, so we grab a baseball bat and a hammer and the five of us kick it and take turns swinging the tools; Ian's the one who finally cracks the glass in the front, and we're all cheering until a cop pulls up, silent, with the lights of his car flashing and asks us what we're doing, and none of us answer, but then he sees Nipple's Mom: in a bathing suit top and cut-offs, framed by the doorway, who yells "Oh, hey Jim!" and smiles, offering one of her cold beers to the uniformed man who greets her on the stoop with a wink, and soon enough he's following her inside to watch the game, and we're already bored with the broken television, now an electronic mess all over the shoulder of the road, so we throw the hammer back in the shed, but keep the baseball bat, and walk around looking for something else to break.

New Rollerskates

ERIN DIONNE

Mrs. Peterson paid Margot a quarter every day to push the buzzer to the Petersons' apartment if Mr. Peterson came home early. Margot Twitter sat on the front steps of her apartment building, flipping the quarter over and over in her fingers, watching. Mr. Peterson was coming down the street, early. He was walking stiffly, as though he had Popsicle sticks for legs, and his hands were balled fists. Margot had been watching for Mr. Peterson for 160 days. She saved 159 quarters to prove it. They pooled, shiny silver, in a bowl next to her bed in apartment 5D. With the forty dollars, twenty dollars per foot, Margot was going to buy new rollerskates.

Mrs. Peterson was inside with Stanley, the building's handyman. Margot knew sex was going on up there. She chewed on the end of her pigtail. Her bedroom was right below the Petersons', and she knew that if she were in there she would hear the bedsprings creaking. Little groans, too.

She could see Mr. Peterson's red face now. He was scowling. Margot stood next to the buzzers, fingers lightly tracing the one for 6D. Mr. Peterson passed her in a surly gust of wind. The front door slammed. Margot Twitter took her hand away from the buzzer, pocketed the quarter, and sat back down on the steps. New rollerskates.

The Last Word

KIRSTEN CULBERTSON

"She's gone," says my father, hanging up the phone. "Heart stopped and she dropped right there in the kitchen. *Thunk*," he says, imitating the way my sister's body must have sounded when it hit the floor.

"For Christ sake," says my mother, sitting down with a hiss. She looks at me, her eldest, standing in my wedding dress in the pastor's office. I am pulling at the zipper that holds me in tight, so tight I can barely breathe now, but my mother takes both of my hands in hers and says, "Look, young lady, first things first."

"She's dead," I say. "Did you hear?"

My father holds both hands over his ears, trying to shut out the voices—not ours, but the ones that circle like whispered lies in his head.

My mother slaps him the way a doctor slaps a newborn to make him breathe. "Tell her," she says. "Tell her we have to be practical."

"You're not serious," I say.

"You better believe I am," says my mother, reaching into the cooler she's stashed under the pastor's desk. "Your relatives haven't spent their retirement money to fly up here for nothing." She cracks open a cold Schlitz and takes a few deep slugs.

"Fuck you," I say, under my breath, but it's loud enough for her to hear. She takes a swing at me, sloshing Schlitz on my father, who just stares out the window at the ocean of wheat that sways in the wind.

"Jesus," I say, jumping one step closer to the door.

"Don't you *Jesus* me," she says and makes a grab for the lace sash at my waist, but I am halfway out the door and down the stairs before she can say another word.

She yells at my father to catch me as I run through the church kitchen to the pantry and find the sheet cake on a shelf. Digging my fingers into the cool, white frosting, I fill my mouth one handful after another. My sister wasn't like me. She ate nothing, while I eat everything and if the devil were here right now I would beg him to play *Let's Make a Deal* so we could swap my mother for my sister because that would only be fair. When my sister and I were tomboys, we played Indians in the woods. We streaked dirt in horizontal stripes across our foreheads and cheeks and made up chants to make the rain fall. I scoop a handful of frosting and streak it across my face in memory of her, but my mother finds me before I can finish and she screams like a woodchuck stuck in one of Uncle Al's traps.

"Now you've done it," she says, "not even Dell will marry you looking like that," and this makes her cry harder than I've seen her cry before. I shove past her out the door that opens into the cemetery, making a beeline for the fir trees that border the edge of the lawn. Their branches scratch my face and tear at the sleeves of my dress as I force myself deeper and deeper into the brush, but I keep running because this is my day and she is my sister and her story won't end any other way.

Huldi (India, 1990)

TARA L. MASIH

Day 1, twilight

Surrounded by voices murmuring, laughing, and giggling as skin makes unaccustomed contact with her. She is the center of it all, sari radiating from her anointed body in iridescent petal folds. Women—relatives, friends, neighbors—hover about in a hum like honeybees eager to stroke and gather. What do they want? she wonders. What is that in their eyes? She is expected to be pale, fey, to keep her eyes modestly downcast, but she looks up through her lashes into Aunty's eyes. She is not sure, but thinks she sees a sadness or a weariness behind the dark-mirrored pupils. In an old neighbor's yellowing eyes she sees a craving, as if smoothing her preconnubial skin will smooth the neighbor's skin, bring something back to life. The handfuls of dough roll up her arms, calves, face, the aromatic oil hypnotizing. Resistant at first, coiling back at first, not used to being touched, she gradually gives in, tension draining. Someone is beating rhythmically on a drum; her heart begins to follow.

Day 2, dusk

She gives herself up more quickly. It is easier to play the timid bride-to-be tonight. She is leaving home in two days. Leaving Mama, Papa, Sarita, and her dog, who barks at mountain lions and keeps her awake at night. Leaving her room with its cot and dresser and movie pictures pasted to the walls. Leaving the garden where she reads, cosmos and marigolds from the States as bright as small suns. Leaving to live at her in-laws' home, in a bedroom prepared for her. She will be their obedient daughter. Someone is dancing and singing. She opens her eyes. Everything is distant, fewer people than yesterday. She watches tea and *laddus* being passed. They are her favorite sweet, but she turns her head when Sarita puts one to her lips. She looks at her own skin, and it is someone else's skin, being smoothed and buffed and colored by the mustard oil and turmeric she'd mixed into chickpea flour. Extra turmeric speeds up the coloring process. Mama remarks on how fair her skin is becoming. She hears the voice, but it is coming from far away.

Day 3, night

She gives herself up completely. The *mahandi* is painted onto her hands and feet. The henna paste is green but will leave a red stain. The swirls wind like snakes around her palms and fingers, up her wrists. She likes the feel of the soft brush caressing her skin. A place at the base of her spine tingles pleasantly. She will wash on the morning of her wedding day. Wash away the green paste and the layers of oil from three nights of *huldi*. The women leave and Mama comes in, closing the curtain. Mama removes her sari, petticoat, bodice. Rubs her whole body—her back, stomach, breasts, thighs. Her match is outside in the garden, eating and drinking in celebration. She is not to see him until tomorrow. His laugh floats through the garden, along the strings of a sitar, into her open window. She closes her eyes, imagines that Mama's hands are his.

A Modern Short Story

STEVE HIMMER

A quirky yet believable character was presented in such a way as to garner sympathy and interest from readers. The character lived in a world familiar to his or her audience, under conditions not unlike their own. This character was by all reasonable measures a good person, but subject to the troubling doubts and desires common to life in our time. When this character met unexpected but not exceedingly dire circumstances in the form of a minor disruption to daily routine, he or she was led to reassess a complicated past decision. This decision had been in large part responsible for the character's arrival at the position he or she currently occupied, perhaps in the form of romance or a job. Whether the choice made in the past had been correct or not remained ambiguous, although the character felt largely satisfied with the outcome of his or her decision and the opportunities it had delivered. In the end, little changed in the character's material situation. The reader was left with a feeling of positive if abstract growth, and avoided the lingering sense of mistruth that accompanies a too-tidy resolution in fiction.

315 WORDS

Directions to Minus World

JOHN F. KERSEY

On the way out of town if you should pass through a yellow, kiss your fist and punch the ceiling. Though you are credibly safe if you do not see the light turn red before you pass under, it never hurts to have some further insurance.

Don't light things with a white lighter. Anything. The stakes are simply too high. And though I don't know the rules concerning lighters that are covered in a plastic wrapping (depicting, for example, a twelve-point buck emerging from the forest), I try to avoid them; beneath the cover, the lighter is white. There is a danger in neglecting to take this single precaution.

If you find that you need time to rest, make sure that all electrical devices in the room, alarm clock notwithstanding, are disengaged from their circuits entirely. Unplug the fuckers. All that extra science in the air is potential dream contaminant. Besides, if you're anything like me you will hear its high pitched whine, and stir all night in your bed.

If for some reason you slap or in any way apply force to your left thigh, make sure you do the same to your right. It is equally important to make sure that both the number of slaps and the firmness of the slaps remain symmetrically equivalent, and your body balanced. If you lose count, slap both of your thighs as many times as possible over the course of, say, a minute. This increases the total number of slaps received on both sides in your lifetime and minimizes the percentage of error accrued by your recent miscalculations.

Write it down or you will lose it. Water saves.

When you reach the sewer, go to the exit pipe and follow my

instructions. They're written down on a napkin, tacked to my wall. I'll send them to you. Mine will be the envelope with the upside-down stamp.

SPECIAL

LAUREL DILE KING

Nina stroked the gum on the underside of her desk lid. The ridges and indentations of the wad were as perfect as the twin, powdery pink rectangles she had unwrapped from their comic moments ago. Now that the class had recited the Pledge of Allegiance and unbowed their heads from the moment of silence, Miss Jacobs would leave the warmth of the radiator and return to the blackboard. Then Nina could pop the gum back in her mouth. Tiny chews were all she dared, because in second grade, if caught with gum, you wore it on the end of your nose. Going cross-eyed to see the gum on your nose made you look retarded and the other kids giggled and pointed. But Nina needed her gum. Her father told her she was like a baseball player—a good chew kept her loose.

While Nina waited for the clickety-click of Miss Jacobs' shoes on the wooden floor, the desk lid grew heavy on her wrist. The room ballooned up with waiting air, like it did when everyone had finished their arithmetic worksheet, except Nina, who still sniffed the cool purple ink, fresh from the mimeograph. The quiet buzzed like when it was Nina's turn to read the Dick and Jane story aloud and she couldn't find her place. Time stuttered, like when the teacher called on her and she couldn't remember five plus eight, while everyone else waved their hands in the air. *Oh! Pick me! I know!*

Nina withdrew her arm from the desk and rested her chin on her shoulder. Back at the radiator, Miss Jacobs whispered to a large woman with gray pin curls. Mrs. Lydol, the Special teacher. Her tennis shoes must have let her slip in during the moment of silence.

The Special class mixed together grades one through five. The Special students had dirty hair or wore the same outfit every day or talked like they had fat tongues. They ate together at a Special table in the cafeteria and yakked with their mouths full. The older kids called it the retard table.

Nina's father said retard was an ugly word that she must never use.

Mary Kay Rogers was a Special—the fat girl with boobies who forgot to flush. Nina had entered the stall right after the red-faced Mary Kay bolted past her and out of the girls' room, without washing her hands. Free of toilet paper, the porcelain bowl showcased the length and breadth of what Mary Kay had left behind. Nina backed out of the stall and bumped into Bonnie Winger, next in line. Bonnie pushed open the door. "Ooo! Yucka cucka!" She leaned forward on tiptoes. "I bet it's long enough to reach through the pipes, all the way to the boys' toilets." Two fourth grade girls, who had been washing their hands, crowded into the stall. "It was that *Special* girl," one of them said. They held their noses, though surprisingly, it didn't stink. There was only the normal muted smell, like a diaper pail, and the scent of wet, brown paper towels. By the afternoon restroom break, all the girls of Main Street School had witnessed Mary Kay's enormous turd. Next morning it had disappeared—either flushed by a teacher, plunged by the janitor, or escaped to the boys' room.

The radiator clanked at the back of the room and the two teachers leaned closer together. Outside, a sliver of sun bounced off the snow-covered branches and sliced through the window to make Miss Jacobs' hair glow like copper. Nina hoped her grown-up hair would look just like that.

Miss Jacobs smiled at Mrs. Lydol, not the smile she saved for the boys with the perfect worksheets, but the tight smile that she wore whenever Nina came for help after school, when none of the other kids were there to make fun of her. No matter how long Nina had to wait, she never said a word until Miss Jacobs looked up from her books and papers. The bright red lips smiled and smiled, but never asked what Nina needed. The teacher made Nina do the asking. Tuesday Nina had needed help weaving her potholder. Whenever she tried to stretch a loop across the frame, another loop popped off. Miss Jacobs made her pull them all off and start over. The frame was still in Nina's desk, loops correctly strung from tooth to tooth, but none woven in yet. Like a little square harp with red strings.

Finally Miss Jacobs finished with the Special teacher and walked up the aisle next to Nina. Nina sat erect, ready to snatch her gum as soon as the teacher passed by. Clickety-click, clickety-click, clickety . . . clunk. Miss Jacobs cleared her throat. Caught? Nina wrinkled her nose in anticipation of the weight of the gum.

"Nina, honey, I'd like you to get your things from your desk." Miss Jacobs spoke so nicely . . . maybe she wasn't caught after all. "Mrs. Lydol is going to be your new teacher."

No. Nina always had clean hair and clean underpants. Miss Jacobs was mad at her because she asked for help so many times. She wanted to get rid of her. What if she had to sit next to Mary Kay Rogers? How would she eat her lunch while everyone stared?

Nina scanned the classroom. All heads were bowed, probably praying that they would never have to eat with the Specials. They would point her out in the lunchroom. *There's Nina. She used to be one of us but now she's a retard*. What would her father say when he found out Nina was an ugly retard?

Nina lifted her desk lid high enough to slide her books out, careful not to expose the gum. A hand on her shoulder made her drop her spelling book. It slid back into the metal bowl of the desk.

Mrs. Lydol—those sneakers again. "You won't need those. We have special books," she said. "Just gather your personal belongings."

The gum was her personal belonging, but with a teacher on either side of her, she could only leave with it on the end of her nose. The one thing that belonged to her, free and clear, was the blue hairbrush in the pencil tray. Goodbye yellow pencils and green chunky eraser. Goodbye potholder on the frame that belonged to Miss Jacobs. Goodbye. Goodbye. Goodbye gum.

Miss Jacobs tapped her pointy black toe. The class shifted in their chairs, whispering. For sure, everybody was sick and tired of Nina taking up so much time.

Miss Jacobs clickety-clicked to the front of the room. "Take out your spelling books, boys and girls."

Mrs. Lydol's hand clamped down on Nina's shoulder. "Come along, dear."

"Come visit us any time, Nina," Miss Jacobs said. "We're just down the hall."

Nina put the hairbrush in her jumper pocket and let Mrs. Lydol steer her toward the door. She paused for one last look at Miss Jacobs. She had written f-r-i-e-n-d on the blackboard. "Our first word is *friend*. Our *friend* Nina moved to a new class. *Friend*."

After Nina was gone, Miss Jacobs would clean out her desk and discover the gum. She would pull it off with a piece of coarse paper towel. Poor gum. Everyone would gawk at what Nina had left behind—all those teeth marks, all those germs. *We thought she might be a retard and now we know for sure.* Then the paper towel would be crumpled and thrown in the trash. No!

Mrs. Lydol put her arm around Nina to sweep her out the door. Nina ducked the arm, marched back to her desk, and opened it wide. The eyes of the class were on her as she peeled off the gum. Miss Jacobs held a piece of chalk in the air, as if she had been assigned an impossible arithmetic problem. Nina chewed. Bazooka forever.

"Come on now, Nina," Mrs. Lydol said. "You're a good girl. Don't make me get Mr. Stockwell." Lydol could just wait and so could the principal.

Nina rolled the gum against her bottom teeth. Ready. She thrust her tongue forward and inhaled deeply.

Out came a bubble the size of a dodge ball. The class gasped. Nina blew a gentle stream of air to keep the bubble inflated. Then she gave it all she had. Pop!

There goes Nina. She sure blows one mean bubble.

How To Set a House on Fire

STACE BUDZKO

Before you light the gas, light a cigarette under the old red maple in the front yard, under a hunter's moon, and take a last look. Before this, walk through the ranch house with a miner's lamp and pesticide sprayer topped off with high-test racing fuel. Before it was your house it was your father's house and before it was your father's house it was his father's too. Before foreclosure on the family farm, before the new highway. Spray the gaps in the oak floorboards and get in the heating ducts, hit the horse-hair plaster and take out electric sockets, then run a heavy gas line out to the barn. There is the combine. That is a backhoe. At one time chickens lived here. Before leaving, make sure the hay bales drip with fuel. This was feed once. On your way toss your house keys into the water well. Before doing anything, make a wish.

After filling the birdbath next to the old red maple with the remaining octane call Herm up at the fire station. After he gets on the line tell him to come over and bring a truck or two—with crew. There's not much to see now, really. After he asks why, tell him. Say how the fire line went from where you stand to the well and then zigzagged to the barn and after the farm equipment blew to the sky tell him how the furnace did the same. A chain of events, explain, it was a chain of events. After the windows kicked out there wasn't much anyone could have done. And after Herm asks if you would do it all over again, tell him you would. But come anyway, Herm. Tell him that.

How To Burn a House

AMY L. CLARK

I used to live with you near two convenience stores and a large plastic cow. The guide books would have said "the beautiful Allegheny River." But what I remember is this. The town was on fire that year. It started with the Tierneys' barn; it was lightning, but that must have been what gave everyone the idea. Three dead cars went up after that, two smoldering down to twisted hulls in lawns on side streets; the third was merely singed by the time some zealous volunteer firemen from the high school screeched up. Some farmers burned their crops as prayer or penance, but possibly they do this every year. The trailer on widowed Mrs. Boulier's property burned from the inside out, wooden cabinets and old linoleum curling the kitchen into nothing around the more durable corrugated aluminum. She got a small amount of insurance money for that, though everyone knew she hadn't touched it since she built her split-level then took the wheels off. Of course some smaller stuff, chimneys and appliances, the usual grease spatters like tiny firework bursts. When the kids tried to do that cow, the accelerant burned so quickly the plastic spots and one of the big, sad, plastic eyes were the only things really melted. Some people said it gave her a wise look. We were, at the time, unclear about the difference between the meteor shower in August and stars dying. We thought that, like a light bulb when the filament is giving up, stars would burn brightest at the end. But it was the river behind the blanket factory that burned most brilliantly against the gray sky that fall, too late in the day for the foliage to compete and not yet dark. It must have been the dye in the runoff, in the wastewater. Flames high and hot and clear, all the colors of dreams.

(for Scott Thomson)

Implosion

MELISSA MCCRACKEN

"Spontaneous combustion," he says. We're on the couch in my apartment and he is braiding, unbraiding, rebraiding my hair. I laugh. Spontaneous combustion sounds funny—calls up an image of his thin body bursting in a "poof," leaving only wispy smoke trails to drift skyward. In truth, it is probably a messy death, but I can't shake the image of him just disappearing.

He is telling me how he would like to die if he could choose. "Maybe a meteor falling on my head," he says. I think of cartoon cats crushed by space boulders that have been pulled to earth by wicked mice. The shocked look on the cats' faces just before impact always cracks me up.

I say that I want to slip away quietly in my sleep. I almost add "alone" but think better of it. I shift around on the couch, present him my feet for a massage. He says, "Front page headlines . . . blaze of glory . . . infamy."

I shake the braid from my hair, toss my head, tease him with the wordless promise of hair in his eyes, across his chest, in his mouth. "How about implosion?" I ask, which I immediately regret. I already know that he will die of a broken heart.

Local Woman Gets a Jolt

JENNIFER PIERONI

It wasn't until lightning struck Michaela that she realized she married an idiot. She was running out in bare feet, to get the mail during a thunderstorm. August was full of storms in Porter County, but then again, so was Michaela. The rain and boom were terminal conditions, as were the flash and cracking of trees and Michaela's knuckles as she sat at the kitchen table with her calculator, ledger, and checkbook.

Her husband, Ron, wouldn't be home from work for another hour, Michaela realized, as she lay flat but electrified on the front lawn, which needed a mow. Michaela saw that the lightning lit the evening the same way the spark of Ron's cigarette lighters had briefly illuminated his face, after sex twenty years ago. She remembered Ron, in his prime, in his youth, with his flashy smile and wanted expression. With his bright girls, light girls, and twenty-eight positions out back of Mighter's field.

The pelting rain rinsed the thought from Michaela's mind. It washed over the grass and soil and, in time, would flood the basement, Michaela knew. As well as she knew the sound of Ron, down there, with the sump pump and a beer, cursing the cracking foundation of their home and God, for the August storms.

Reaching Fever

DERRICK ABLEMAN

Officially, magnetic fields know of no acting king or monarch, but their lives are legislated all the same by metals and poles and small pockets of charge that command their constant reach and drag. This is not considered a tyranny among the fields, who have nothing otherwise to do and so welcome the work, finding a kind of brotherhood in the towing of things. Each wave in the field is expected to do his part, some going out in front, for the gathering, while still others remain behind, lending support.

"The labor is equal. Each to his part," as the outer waves sometimes say. Only they can speak, being spread so far from their source and home charge, out to distant lands where the fields loosen into distinct waves. There, in these distances, each wave becomes capable of feeling his own travel and knowing himself, for once apart from the charge.

But of this they never tell the others when they return and reabsorb, some game in tow or else entirely repulsed, tired and glad for the rest. They never breathe a word of it, this separateness, for each wave becomes large-hearted by the knowledge—lonely too—and this they decide, in the few moments they feel it, is a weight and a curse. So they always turn back when they hear themselves think, sometimes before finding anything. They turn back and chase themselves home, forgetting it each time they collapse into one another.

But some nights, at the edges of sleep, on the tops and bottoms of the waking world, there are dreams that skip across the fields like stones, raising ripple pools of plots and plans. Some think (and the thinking spreads) that tomorrow morning they could all push out from the source and dissolve into space, each allotted a few moments of life before negation. But escape is impossible; deep as knowing going they all know this. The source is the source and will drag them back, no matter the distance.

Still, there are rumors. At the poles, where the sources are the strongest and the waves so thick they border on visibility, here there are rumors of another charge, a greater charge so like a god that the poles themselves circle in worship. A Sun Charge, hot heart of all charges, Father of all Fields.

At the poles the plan evolves—slowly, as each out-going wave is given only moments of privacy to plot before it's drawn back, its work forgotten. But ever-steady, the plans return to the fields in the form of dreams, each night building on the back of the last, until they learn to dream while waking, becoming of one mind.

They are aiming for the Sun. Selecting waves and dispatching them like prayers. Some will perish or be repulsed—they know this. Many will simply disintegrate, few will find it and fewer still will bear the time alone, the agony of their own voices echoing through space. But some will make it, remembering their mission, aged centuries by the travel and exile. These are the ones now so different from their kin that they can be seen, even from here, surrounding the Sun, burning up in the bliss of forgetting.

WHAT I HAVE TO REMEMBER

MARY SALIBA

Three years ago, dad gave me a terrible coat Christmas morning. That night, after lemon butter duck and blackberry pie, he died.

My coat is the color swamp. Lima bean wax left for days kind of color. The label says: "comfort Level: -40-50 Degrees, Goose Down." I'm sure it wasn't cheap, even at the Discounted Color Rack Shack in North Conway, where the outlets are.

None of my scarves match it, especially the flamingo pink velour mom bought me for my birthday last June, an out-of-season special at the Route 12 Sale Whale.

My friend Jill says I'm not unattractive. Whenever we go skating, she says I need a different color coat, that's all, for my complexion. It's a good coat, I tell her, good until forty degrees below and she says it never gets that cold and it never will. She stole me her stepmother's *Color Me Right*, which says I need blush tones.

I have seven catalogues in my bedtable drawer. I sneak them upstairs under my shirt when the mail comes. (Mom says no way do we buy from someone you can't look in the eye.) Every night at nine, I lie in bed with a bowl of chocolate chip mint ice cream and look at coats. There's a red Thinsulate with seven pockets and a coyote-lined hood. And a silk one with no warmth at all that just flows. I circled the color "Morning Swan," and "Cinnamon Tea" as my second choice.

But it's my father keeping me warm. I have to remember that.

This Is How I Remember It

ELIZABETH KEMPER FRENCH

Watching Joey pop the red berries into his mouth like Jujubes at the movies and Mags only licking them at first, then chewing, so both of their smiles look bloody and I laugh although I don't eat even one . . . then suddenly our moms are all around us (although mine doesn't panic until she looks at the others, then screams with them things like *God dammit did you eat these?* and shakes me so my "No" sounds like "oh-oh-oh") and then we're being yanked toward the house, me for once not resisting as my mother scoops me into her arms, and inside the moms shove medicine, thick and purple, down our throats in the bathroom—Joey in the toilet, Mags in the sink, me staring at the hair in the tub drain as my mom pushes my head down, and there is red vomit everywhere, splashing on the mirror and powder blue rugs, everywhere except the tub where mine is coming out yellow, the color of corn muffins from lunch, not a speck of red; *I told you*, I want to scream, and then it is over and I turn to my mother for a touch or a stroke on the head like the other moms (but she has moved to the doorway and lights a cigarette, pushes hair out of her eyes) and there is only her smeared lips saying, *This will teach you anyway*.

927 WORDS

The ABCs of Family History

ASHLEY RICE

A man lost his hand once on my grandfather's farm. Before they could get the man to any help (a nearby farmhouse) the hand had already turned blue. "Careful. Careful!" my father (a child then) had warned, as Jesse reached into the machine to pull out a tangle of grass, but it was already too late. Dead-on-arrival (in modern terms) is what the hand was termed. Everyone: the animal doctor, his neighbor, my father, my grandmother, everyone tried to revive that hand, as if it were the last hand in America, because Jesse was screaming, because the hand had turned blue, because there weren't a lot of farm hands around to harvest the wheat that year, but it was already too late. From this I gathered that it's not the best idea to stick your hand into a running piece of machinery, but people sometimes did.

Going over stories from my family's past, as a kid, in an attempt to explain my parents' behavior to myself, was something I sometimes did.

Harder to pin down in a single thought at the beginning of a story are the greater implications of why we are the way we are, do the things we do, or even cling to stories at all, but, one day, around age 11, I, Kelly Anderson, began.

I figured out a lot through books, or secondhand: if a grown (and married) woman was a witness to a field-machine related tragedy back then, I learned, then you knew that things had gone from bad to worse, that your grandfather had been sick, and your grandmother and father had been out working the fields again, when your father should have been miles away in school.

Killings, non-accidental violence, etc.—to begin with—were ways you got money: the slaughtering of hogs, the shooting of farm dogs who could not be fed is what farmhands did, and yes, Kennedy, I knew from history class, would soon be president, but "at home," in backwoods country, there was still no bathroom. Home-life, my father decided, belonged someplace different, and so he began to study arithmetic books like a madman to get himself out of there.

My own school picture at 10 years old (in contrast) would be a childhood of embarrassing lunchbox choices, pigtails and laughter, but was, I'll admit, anchored-in-estrangements-and-gaps, absences-and-things-which-I-could-not-understand.

"Nothing can be learned from what happened in those days, Kelly," my father told me privately, when I was graduating elementary school, packing up my desk, as if, in regards to our Overall Family Story, it was already (which pissed me off) (didn't he see that I was a superhero, like the characters on my lunchbox?) too late.

Once though, on a lark (he was drunk, at my high school graduation) (I was drunk, at my high school graduation) I unearthed more words from him, and I continued to do this direct, hands-on-communication sporadically, when he was not drunk (he usually wasn't) (I usually wasn't, sort of) though the snatches never made sense.

"Perhaps it's better that you know some things about the past, in the end," he conceded to me (I was 21, home from college) when my mother—whose parents had left (this earth) years earlier—was not there. "Questions lead to questions with you, Kelly," he said next, refusing to tell me the rest, offering to take me out to dinner instead.

Retrospectively speaking, dinner at the Mexican Food Restaurant was, for me, The Very End, for, having done my research thoroughly, and simply because I understood my parents better as a result of trying to understand them, I liked my parents by now (I researched my mother, but lack-of-information caused-by-grief often made this harder).

Sometimes, home for Christmas, I'd still hear something which told me a thing or two about who we are/who we were (as Andersons in general), other times I wasn't listening.

Though I wouldn't have said so, my mind still returned in private moments to the cut-off hand of Jesse (a man I never knew, for he'd died that long ago afternoon, nor had I ever heard the end to his story) Until one day, pulled forward by the overarching demands of the end to a millennium, I too finally "left."

Verging on today, I happily catapulted myself into The Land of the Living, which is the only place you learn anything real at all about beginnings, endings, or death, so it's only now, circa the end of the twentieth century, that I know this slightly fictionalized version of "Jesse's Hand" to be true. When there had been an accident once, and my father had not been able to stop a near-senile man from sticking his hand into a machine, my grandfather had called him over and knocked him on the side of the head a time or two with a frying pan, to remind him of the fragileness of life, with the sound of death, a warning, but my father could not hear it, he was 10, his left eardrum had burst on a dive too deep into a lake that summer, by then he was, for a time, half-deaf. Xylophones are what the windchimes must have sounded like on the Anderson Family Farm on that lost day, wild and windmade, lost forever. You would tell a different story, maybe, if you had been there, for what we hand down through the years is like a hand-worn quilt, or a piece of our old selves. Zephrying, then, to the present.

Intelligence

MATT MARINOVICH

I'm eight years old. But I have the mind of a nineteen-year-old. Mom says it's making up for all the wrong Dad did. Today there's going to be a whole camera crew here. They're going to film different angles of me beating myself at chess. Then they want me to walk around the neighborhood in my Eagle Scout uniform. Dad doesn't want to talk to them. So I guess they'll do an exterior of the penitentiary.

Dad called a few hours ago. Mom handed me the phone. She never wants to talk to him. I end up answering all the questions he wants to ask her. He asked me when was the last time Mom talked about him. I told him she said something at the bowling alley because we were having trouble keeping score. Mom doesn't care how much I lie to him because she says he's going to rot in jail. I miss him. But I can't tell him that. Mom would hit the roof and call me a traitor and start the whole thing about who's bringing me up and who's the slob behind bars. With Mom, eventually everything comes down to physical appearances. "It was a choice between your dad and Henry Lee," she says when she reminisces about marrying Dad. "And Henry Lee had hair on his back."

On the phone, I asked Dad what he made in woodshop, and he asked me if I was eating lots of peas and carrots because the brain is just another muscle and you can't feed it junk. Dad thinks he's grooming me for the Nobel Prize. I made a few reading suggestions. I send him books and tell him to highlight the difficult parts. He's not very easy to explain things to. If he doesn't get it the first time, he gets angry—and when he gets angry, he automatically thinks of Mom and says, "Don't sign anything. Not even your homework. I own the rights to you. Every single cent you make, you freak of fucking nature."

I never hang up on him, no matter what he says.

I wait until he calms down, and then give him an update on how many sparrows have moved into the birdhouse we built.

But it's really sitting in the basement.

The camera crew is here. Taping down cable and knocking over chairs. Mom's on the phone right now because the producer wants a shot of me playing with my friends. I told him I could punch up some people on my computer. But he wants the real thing. So Mom's on the phone, asking Mrs. Milgram if she can borrow her son for the afternoon. That's the same kid who smashed up my invention for the Science Fair last year. The key grip is showing me how to throw a Frisbee. The producer is suggesting a shot of me bicycling down Quarry Lane with my dog running after me. But Einstein has arthritis and bleeding gums. He can barely stand up.

The whole neighborhood's watching us. Kids on mountain bikes and skateboards are casing our house, making circles in the road. When Dad was taken away, Mom ran out and aimed the sprinkler at them. Now she's too busy. She's even got a pencil behind her ear.

I tell the producer I know what people want to see. They want to see me in my tiny apron making a white sauce. Or me playing the piano. A little Vivaldi and maybe the camera panning to my sneakers dangling a foot from the floor while my mother turns the pages and presses the pedal. I love it when she steps on the pedal, when the notes run together and take too long to end.

I lower my head and pretend that this is sadness.

This Is How We Learned

JANICE O'LEARY

Huddled together on the steps in the darkness of the stairwell where the railing ended, trying not to let our pajama feet crinkle like tissue paper, we listened to them. Our parents who did not curse said words we heard only on cable TV. We hadn't known that lips which kissed our foreheads and taught us prayers could form the shapes of such anger. Later, or the next day, I pulled her hair; she pinched the backs of my arms or gave me monkey knots at the crook of my elbow. Playing Barbies we'd make them say things: Shit-head, Ken said to Barbie; Ass-face, Barbie said to Ken. Mom didn't hear or see except that once, when she asked where had we learned to treat each other so badly, to use such language. She cried while we sat on the edge of the sink. With the burn of Ivory still in our throats, we said, Fuck you, Mom, enunciating like she always told us to do.

Mimi

JACQUELINE HOLLAND

I covet my neighbor's dog. Nothing about that in the Ten Commandments. Still, I feel guilty. If you saw the little minx you'd understand: a smooth, coppery, long-haired dachshund with the serious face of a banker. Mimi is nine years old, a tulip lover, and sweeter than cinnamon. When I hear the screen door slam, I perch on my window seat and sneak peeks out my pet-less apartment window like a desperate, backward Peeping Tom. Mimi's cruller-like shape, released into the backyard, trots to the garden, fur flouncing like Farrah Fawcett's feathered hair. She sniffs about the tulips, sussing out rabbits, then, as if in answer to my soft humming, she looks up with those marble eyes and grins.

I am an opera singer. I try out new roles on Mimi, my solo, adoring audience.

I don't harbor any tennis balls or playthings under my couch. I don't stock up on Milk-Bones when they're on sale. I don't ever command anything to "Sit," "Stay," or "Come." She knows this—knows that I don't know the vocabulary of dogs. She sees me like an old woman in a nursing home longing for babies, I'm sure. A woman who once had a beautiful voice.

In winter, I am adrift. Mimi dislikes the cold and only scampers out quickly to visit the lifeless lilac bush before darting back inside. I have spent nine long winters here. In summer, I am in love. She lolls about for hours in the shade, blanketing herself in grass freshly cut and lapping softly at her pads, hot from darting down the flagstone path to the garden.

When I practice the scales, I linger a bit on *mi-mi-mi-mi*, though my neighbors have asked me to stop. When I look out to see if Mimi knows I am singing about her, her droopy eyes look upward, intent on spotting my silhouette. I am here, Mimi, I say. And I wave.

BAD DOG

JENNIFER PIERONI

It was a side-of-the-road dog. Seemed to Renee the kind of dog that someone couldn't afford to feed or that someone, drunk, kicked around. "Must've followed me here," she said. "Will you let her stay?" Ben, her husband, knelt next to the dog and smiled as Renee noticed that their tulips were wilting again. Too much water and attention Ben gave them. "Over-tending," Renee called it.

Ben threw a stick for the dog to catch and said "I haven't had a dog since 1982," when he and his brother were followed home by a stray. Their dog, Jeepers, was hit by a car not more than a week after they convinced their father to allow them to keep her. "Sometimes, in dreams, Jeepers still follows me," Ben said.

Renee watched Ben rub the dog's stomach. The word crossed her mind: Loyalty. From where she stood, plucking flimsy, rotting stems from the earth, she felt like a destroyer of all that is good and just in Ben's world.

Sweeping

JOSH PAHIGIAN

Lucy's arms were full. One wrapped around a brown paper grocery bag, holding it up against her chest, while a gallon of spring water weighed down the other. She trudged up the first, then the second, then the third and final flight of stairs. It was Friday night, the end of a long week. She was tired but happy to be home. With her jug-hand, she aimed and inserted the key. She turned gently and pressed the door open.

Somehow Lucy knew. Later, talking to the police, she would point to the spilled bag on the kitchen floor, the broken carton of eggs and broken pickle jar and tell them that somehow she knew. Before she turned on the light, before she saw him standing there, she knew. Knew she was about to be violated.

She recognized him. Neither of them pretended she wouldn't or shouldn't. He was a neighbor. Always out there sweeping—cleaning the 100 feet of sidewalk and street in front of his parents' house. Sweeping away the rain, the snow, the leaves, the fallen apple blossoms, the dog shit. The courtroom report in the paper two days later did not mention the sweeping. It said that he was mentally handicapped and that he was 34 years old.

Lucy did not fear for her life. She was terrified but she did not fear for her life. She had walked past him sweeping too many times for him to kill her. She cried at first then she waited and waited, then finally he was finished and she began to cry again. He pulled his pants up as he walked into the kitchen, then Lucy heard a loud crack and the rush of water falling on linoleum. Then she heard the sound of the door slowly swishing closed, followed by his first few footsteps on the stairs.

Afterwards, talking to the officers, Lucy would shake her head and say, "That sick fuck. He smashed my fish tank with a coffee mug."

ONE DAY WALK THROUGH THE FRONT DOOR

MOLLY LANZAROTTA

It got so the only place I could cry was the freeway since traffic jams and the absence of curves made driving and crying less dangerous, unlike surface streets which scattered the pile of flyers on the passenger seat, jumbling the printed images of my sister's face and frightening me beyond tears the with the sight of a life slipping out of reach as I pulled into gas stations, cafes, rest stops, a mad woman slapping flyers on walls, in people's faces, blurting, *Have you seen her?* . . . until soon I only made calls from phone booths, avoiding the empty apartment I shared with her, talking to police, friends, reporters, even giving phone interviews, so sometimes it was my own voice on the news as I drove, *I just hope she's safe, I want her home,* other times my voice shouted back at the radio, *Say her name, don't drop the story, oh Jesus, please,* then I'd cry more and believe how alone I felt, surrounded by hundreds of people encased in tinted-glass worlds that could neatly hide any individual horror, until I could only whisper, *Please even just her body,* because I had to know or I'd be stranded in this moment forever and I'd never sleep again, but wait, always wait to see her one day just walk through the front door . . . then, finally, my last hope was to hear it from our priest, but it was the car, detached reporting from that radio on the fifth day: they'd found a body, floating in the bay.

Drag

STEVE HIMMER

Every sleeper in the city woke up that morning with a dead body chained to one leg. The links were cold iron, and the cuffs around their ankles were heavy and dark and forged somehow without seams to show how they had been put on. The bodies made showering difficult, jogging impossible, and family dogs all over town snarled and sniffed at stiff strangers invading their floors.

Bodies dragged through their morning as the city dragged through its own, overcrowding coffee counters and leaving bus riders hard-pressed for seats. Elevators stalled when somebody's body wouldn't squeeze through the doors and got hung up on the outside. Airplanes left passengers stranded because attendants were never quite sure how many live persons they'd counted and how many passed on carry-ons. Pedestrians forgot they were walking for two and wondered why their legs were so tired, muscles cramped and backs aching after just a few steps.

The city moved in slow motion past newspaper-box windows flashing fresh photographs from the far front of a war, but most eyes were too tired for headlines.

Children couldn't get through front doors because the adult bodies behind them were too heavy to move. Parents let them stay home from school for the day if they promised not to watch much TV.

Beneath a gold dome on the city's highest hill, politicians charged onto the debating floor only to trip over the deadweight at their feet. No bills were passed, no edicts edicted, and the day piled up in a tangle as lawmakers teased their own bodies apart from the bodies of so many others. City Hall shut down after lunch when it was clear they would get nothing done, and senators spilled onto the street with nothing to do but go home.

Offices were quiet in the late afternoon as worn-out file clerks and CEOs napped off the aches in their laden legs, or else snuck out early, thumping down stairs with their bodies behind. Bodies squeaked across the tiles of supermarket aisles as shoppers too tired to remember what they usually ate pushed carts full of unwanted food. Families passed dinner without one word spoken, just the scraping of forks on mashed potato-piled plates.

Citizens went to bed early that night in droves. Long before the late news they tucked their bodies and chains under the blankets beside them, pushing spouses apart and knocking slumbering pets off the edge of the bed. They slept and they dreamt of their own lives before they dragged bodies behind them.

Lovely

LESLIE BUSLER

As I walked through the door my man said, *Hello, my lovely,* and I thought, *How wonderful*: every day for forty-two years he has greeted me the same way. Bending down to slip off my Dr. Scholl's, I asked my darling what he'd been up to on this very fine afternoon. Cataloging the kitchen staples, he told me. Did I know we had three boxes of Bisquick and six unopened jars of red raspberry preserves? Excellent, I replied, and asked if he might whip us up a delicious surprise. Fidgeting and perplexed, my darling turned to the other items in the pantry as if seriously pondering what he might create using two boxes of Shake 'n Bake, four cans of wax beans, several pounds of sprouting potatoes, and half a dozen beef bouillon cubes. Gordon, our irascible 30-year-old son, was coming to dinner, and it really wasn't right of me to give my sweet forgetting man more of a reason to perspire.

Happiness typically abounded at our small table for two, but the last time Gordon popped in with four hoops along each eyebrow, a tattoo of a maimed torso on his neck, and a crooked little pout on his nice square face, the unsettling ensued. It was, you might say, a ridiculous scene of nerves and failing memory: my darling's being slowly thieved by dementia while our son sat catatonic from whatever thought-altering substance—what's the latest: crank, crack, smack?—he'd bought on the streets. Just imagine the two of them at opposite ends of the table, drooling onto their helpings of tater tot casserole, and there I am in the middle of it all saying, "Gordon, this is your father. Darling, your son."

Knowing, or rather hoping, Gordon would arrive within the hour, I set my darling about the business of setting the table while I poured myself a tiny drink. Liquor for levity I always say, though I do try to keep it to two gin fizzes on an empty stomach. Much to my satisfaction I had stumbled upon a Greek restaurant on the way home from the geriatric clinic, so to avoid having to fry up a chicken I stopped in and bought kielbasa, three squares of baklava, and sixteen ounces of plump Kalamata olives, several of which I partook during the cab ride to counter my blood pressure medicine, which can make me a bit woozy.

Normally at this time I would have insisted we do our evening exercises: I encourage my darling to recite the alphabet forward and back in an attempt to keep his mind sharp while I get out the fencing gear and practice balestras, gracefully launch counter attacks against the menacing floral-print high back. Oh, we are spry in our old age, save for the slipping sense. Procrastinating, however, had become my most recent virtue, and I saw no reason why we couldn't shake those small tasks off for a time.

Queer as it sounds, I had a feeling then, a sense that something with dear Gordy was awry. Rough and tumble as his life was, he'd avoided the predictable: gun shot wounds, evictions, prison, jaundice. Still a mother knows well enough when something's being taken away, and as I sipped my second gin fizz and watched my darling sitting in his wrangled recliner, I felt a cold dig at the heart. Time passed wretchedly slow as we waited (my recently replaced hip made sitting for long stretches dreadful, and my darling was accustomed to eating dinner early, thus he kept putting odd objects in his mouth to ward off starvation), but finally at nine p.m. we devoured the kielbasa and killed the gin along with the fizz, and still Gordon didn't show. Until dawn I sat near the window and watched the gilded city sky slip out of its posh evening gown and into the pink silk it would wear to sleep the wee hours away. Vociferous as Gordon could be, I did still fret for the soft boy he had been when he played the hammered dulcimer back in high school, and as I watched the streets below, I seemed to see my son's many faces mingling with the figures passing along the sidewalks. When day broke and my darling tottered out of the bedroom in his corduroy slippers, kissed me on the forehead, and said, *Hello, my lovely,* I thought, *Here we are again.*

X, you see my little dearies, is the place he kisses me every day of this sweet life, X the spot where our bodies fall and get back up again, X the hour when we hear a rap at the door and find our dearest, our only child, clammy and blue at the threshold whimpering, Mummy, Daddy, Mum. You think these sorts of thing aren't going to happen in your banal little world. Zoom in and take a closer look, dearie: this is it, your life, and you do the best you can.

I Invented the Moonwalk (and the Pencil Sharpener)

BRAIIAN RUUSKA

I'm not the most sympathetic guy, but even I felt remorse over Zane Gunderson's passing. It didn't end well for him at all.

As a wide-eyed young man of twenty-three, Zane was struck by inspiration and invented the pencil sharpener, for which he was universally praised. In fact, for the next forty years, he did little more than walk around town with his hands in his pockets, smiling contentedly as he watched young men write love letters to their sweethearts, or mothers write to their daughters who were finding happiness in the big city, or old men write complaints to a biscuit factory or a dungaree warehouse or a butter-churn repository, and their pencils would snap from applying too much pressure. A momentary look of distress would flash across their faces, but then they'd reach into their knapsack or purse and produce one of those newfangled pencil sharpeners. After a few twisting motions, they'd resume writing as if nothing had happened and Zane would continue on his way with a warm feeling in his heart. That's what got the lonesome bachelor through his days.

This continued until he was diagnosed with arthritis at the age of sixty-three. Soon it became agonizing for him to even walk, so he lay in bed all day, sullen over being deprived of the only joy he had.

One day, Zane was in his kitchen and discovered that if he walked backwards, sliding his feet stylishly as he did so, he was able to move without pain. He joyfully threw his grilled cheese sandwich against the wall and headed into the center of town.

As usual, people were seated on benches or on the ground,

writing letters, poems, or lists of what they were grateful for. When they saw Zane's distinctive walk, each of their pencils broke at once. As one, they stood and imitated him, despite the old man's frenzied pleas that they ignore him, that they sit down, sharpen their pencils, and continue to write. No one listened.

Hardly any writing went on around here during Zane's miserable final years on earth, so thoroughly did people enjoy this "moonwalk" he'd unwittingly invented. All five of the local pencil sharpener stores went out of business.

I sat in a chair next to Zane's deathbed as his final moments passed. I reminded him of the good times we'd had, but he just kept insisting that his headstone read, "Inventor of the Pencil Sharpener," and make no mention of the moonwalk, but I think he knew that would be impossible.

My friend's last words, as his lungs filled with the black fluid, were, "I envy you, Thomas." He envied me, and do you know what my contribution to society was? You know how fast-food restaurants provide you with those little packets of ketchup? Well, it was my idea to put a little perforated line where you should tear the packet open. That's all I ever did.

Winter

CHRISTOPHER HELMUTH

This old man comes up the alley toward our fire. His hair is as white and as wild as any of ours, but his clothes are clean, and he's wearing patent leather shoes.

"Listen, gentlemen," he says flatly. "I have a favor to ask."

With both hands, the old man gently holds a small wooden box. He says he's lived a full and rich life. Says he had a pleasant childhood. His parents never attended school, yet sent him to Yale Law. He won case after case, became the youngest associate, partner, councilman. He says he fell in love, married, had three wonderful children and a spacious townhouse. Cherished his life more with each passing day.

Then, he says, life turned on him. His youngest daughter was killed in an auto accident. His oldest, raped in the woods and left to die. His son was diagnosed with leukemia and lasted only six more months.

His wife eventually stopped eating. Wouldn't leave the house. She was easily confused: she couldn't always remember her husband's name or what had happened to her children. He had to tell her, again and again and again.

At this point, the old man says, he'd had enough. He'd made his decision. He reached deep down into himself with both hands and pulled up all his emotions—the joy of his son's birth, the fear of his neighbor's Dobermans, the wonder of his wife's naked body—everything, in great congealed gobs of sentiment, his anger joined with his melancholy joined with his exaltation joined with his shame. The old man reached down again and again until he was completely empty, until all that remained was this wet, jiggling mass of feelings on the desk in front of him. He dumped everything into a shoebox, looped a rubber band over the lid, and slid the box under his bed.

His life improved, he says. He was able to sleep, to perform his daily routine with cool dexterity. He could easily be amiable to the old woman who shared his bed, could feed her, could bathe her, could look at her decimated frame without a hint of sadness.

Soon, though, a stench rose from under the bed. The emotions had soaked the thin cardboard of the box and were leaking through its disintegrating walls. The man began to feel hints of affection toward his wife, and instead of finding another box, the old man breathed in the feelings, basking in their forgotten warmth. But the more deeply he inhaled, the darker his sentiments grew. He was brought lower and lower, he says, until finally he gathered the strength to once again box up the lot of it.

It was foolishness, the old man says, but knowing his feelings were under the bed, he couldn't keep himself from them. Each time he opened the box he reveled more completely in its contents, and on each occasion his binges left him more hopeless, more desolate, and more broken. During this last episode he'd been so thoroughly at the will of his emotions that he'd spent an entire morning wailing at the gravestones of his children. He knew then he needed not only to box up his feelings, but to rid them from his house, to rid them from his life forever.

"That," the old man says, "is what I'm asking of you gentleman." He gives us fifty dollars each to take his coffin full of feelings and give it a proper burial someplace where it will not be found, not by him, not by anyone. The contents of that box are extremely valuable, he says, they are his life, but they can only cause harm if they're let loose. He looks us right in the eye when he says this. We all nod. He hands us the box solemnly, then heads back down the alley.

As soon as he's around the corner we open up the box. We take out his emotions, cook them up in our pan, and eat them whole. We throw the wooden box on our fire and warm our freezing hands. "This has got to be the coldest January ever," someone says.

Pictures of Children Playing

ROBERT REPINO

Miles was thinking about his baby girl when he spotted the dead soldier.

The body lay in a crater carved out of the gravel in the back of the smashed school building. Rubble from the crumbling cinderblock wall had fallen on the corpse, covering him with gray soot and pebbles.

Miles looked away for a second, and saw Sergeant Travis behind him, crouching in the doorway, clutching his rifle. Miles looked up at the sky—which he could see through the hole in the ceiling—and tried to get his daughter's face back into his mind. He wanted to think about that Christmas morning, when his wife playfully yelled at him for giving their daughter the jersey. She had gone to Michigan. But they were all gone from his mind, locked out for a bit, and he had no choice but to look down at this dead boy in front of him.

He stepped forward and stared at the body. The face was gray, the mouth frozen into a crooked scream. Dark brown blood matted the soldier's shirt, mercifully hiding the name stenciled on the chest. The corpse reclined in the crater, his legs spread so that the dirty boots pointed to two and ten o'clock. If you put a beer in his hand, Miles thought, he would look like he was relaxing in a lawn chair.

Some gunfire in the distance made Miles drop to his knees suddenly. He heard the sergeant laughing behind him. Travis had always told them, "You might as well stay standing, dumbass—if you can hear it, it's already passed. Or you're already dead."

Crouching, Miles was only a couple of feet from the dead man. He could smell the beginnings of decomposition, or at least thought he could. Miles tried to find anything in the room he could look at besides the body, and found a row of drawings still tacked to the wall beside him. They were pictures of children playing, the young artists' names signed in some alien language at the bottom.

Miles suddenly remembered what he had been thinking about a moment earlier. He clenched his eyes shut and pictured Christmas morning with his family. "Oh, you think you're funny?" his wife had asked him as he carried his daughter around the room in her little jersey, singing the Notre Dame fight song while she looked into his eyes and giggled.

Then Miles wondered what the dead man had thought about earlier that day.

A thud came from the front door of the little school. Miles tensed his muscles to get up and run just as the explosion roared towards him, shaking the entire world, tumbling him over, propelling him backward, tearing up the earth and walls around him.

Travis shook his head to get the ringing out of his ears. He stood up, and watched the dust and debris slide off of his shoulders and arms. The wall he had used as a barricade had been chopped in half, its remains spilled across the floor. Travis headed toward the back of the school, trying to remember what he was thinking about right before the explosion. This always happens, he thought.

And then it came back to him. He was thinking about fishing with his brother the previous summer, when he had told his brother that he was shipping out for real this time. Travis imagined his brother holding a trout in one hand and a beer in the other when he spotted Miles, lying face down, his dead arms stretched out in front of him.

A Case for Sterner Prison Sentencing and Reflections on a Personal Tragedy By Bear

HEATHER QUARLES

My therapist says it's useless to dwell on what might have been, but I can't help wondering how our story might have turned out different if the cottage had had a decent security system—a burglar alarm, or at least some functional locks on the doors. Or for that matter if Goldilocks had never broken into our house at all—if we'd never laid eyes on those corkscrew curls, the pasty little face, or that dress with the sappy blue pinafore. What would our lives be today if she hadn't violated our home six years ago bringing everything, as they say in therapy, to "crisis"?

I remember that fateful morning as if it were yesterday. We'd been out gathering berries—Papa Bear, Mama Bear, and I—and had returned to find the cottage door standing open. I told my mom "don't go in" but she didn't listen; she had a can of Mace in her apron and felt she could handle the situation. (They didn't put that in the article, those damn reporters. They made it sound like we just stumbled in unarmed, like morons, and went around gawking at all the broken furniture—you know, "Someone's been eating my porridge," "Someone's been eating *my* porridge," "Someone's broken my chair" etc., etc.—until we came face to face with Goldilocks herself in the bedroom.) The truth is we were very cautious, although in retrospect we should have dialed 911 and waited for the police to arrive before we entered the building.

Immediately after Goldilocks was apprehended and word got

out to the media, we got swamped with calls—especially me because it was my stuff that was damaged. I still remember the throngs of reporters, the flashbulbs, the questions, "Baby Bear, how does it feel to have your chair broken, your breakfast tampered with, your bed slept in by a complete stranger, a criminal off the street? How did you feel that first moment when you realized your porridge was missing?"

Dad and Mom managed to stay in the background at first. Papa Bear was distant in those days anyway. I guess if I hadn't been so young and stupid I would have seen the signs of marital instability—his mysterious bouts with chronic hibernation, the fact that as long as I can remember, he and Mama Bear slept in separate beds. Looking back, of course I can see how dysfunctional our cottage was, but then I was blind to it all. It took me completely by surprise when six months after the break-in he left with some dancing-bear bimbo who'd escaped from a Grateful Dead concert. They migrated to Hollywood and we've only heard from Dad once since then—a postcard bragging that he got a contract with Disney for the Grizzly scene in *Wilderness Family, Part Four*. No child support check enclosed, nothing.

Then there was Mom, poor Mama Bear. I think the whole thing hit her the hardest. She didn't have much of a life in those days, see—that modest hut in the forest was her whole world. Her self-esteem was rooted there and our daily routines gave her a sense of empowerment. When Goldilocks came along, all that was shattered. The house was in disarray, breakfast shot to hell, the neighbors scandalized. She's never been the same since, and it's merely salt in her wound to know that Goldilocks is now up for parole.

According to the lawyers, she'll be free in less than a month. She's already scheduled appearances on three different TV shows: *Jenny Jones, 20/20,* and *A Current Affair*. And to top it off, I've just been informed that the weasely reporter who broke this story has sold the rights to Little Golden Books. We'll never live down the publicity—he's ruined our lives, this no-name, this hack. Calls himself the Narrator. What an asshole.

I've relived it a million times in therapy, but I still want to puke remembering the look on that kid's face when we walked in on her in my bed. *My* bed. She sat up with her hair all tousled and gave us this innocent victim look, a child seeking refuge from the dark forest, and it worked. It stopped Mama Bear in her tracks, she put that Mace right back in her apron. (I know she's since wished she'd blinded the little delinquent.) It worked on the media too, and the jury, and the judge. Goldilocks ended up with half the prison sentence she deserved. And now, in one month, she'll be at large.

My therapist keeps saying, "Bitterness helps no one. It's merely a destructive emotion," but lately I am forming my own views on the subject. Between counseling sessions, I've been doing a lot of reading: *Grizzlies in America, Sudden Attack! The Yellowstone Massacre*. None of this "Winnie the Pooh" shit, I'm getting back to my roots and discovering what teeth and claws are for. I'll tell you one thing: Goldilocks had better watch her back.

Abercrombie & Fitch

DON LEE

It's a problem. She only goes out with white guys, he only goes out with blondes. It's the familiar case of Asians believing in their own bad press: they're geeks with small weenies, they're wallflowers with little mystery. Yet with age, they've become curious—perhaps they've been too harsh and narrow-minded all these years—and they accept the date that's been arranged for them by their parents. The date goes all right. Nothing to write home about, but not so terrible, not onerous enough to preclude another dinner. They get drunk and end up on her living room floor, yanking clothes off. Fucking-A, you're huge, she says, and she discards her coolie hat and slaps him so hard, his slanty left eye immediately begins to welt. Fucking-A, you're sick, he says, sinking his bucktoothed mouth into her neck—sallow, tasty—loving it.

PRICKS

SHEEHAN MCGUIRK

After I slammed my pointer finger in the car door last week, I waited for the swelling to go down. At the tip, it is a small but perfect plum. I ask Mickey if he will take me to the emergency room.

"When? Now?" He hangs his jump rope around his neck and checks his heart rate with the gadget I bought for him last Christmas, when we moved in together.

"Today or tomorrow," I say and lean back against the garage door. "You know," he says, "they're going to charge you for sticking a stupid pin in it."

He looks at my finger from across the room, I put my hands behind my back.

"It's giving me headaches," I say. He puts down the jump rope and lies back on the mat with his Abflex.

"Did you take the B-12 I left out for you?" he asks.

"I forgot."

He rolls his eyes in mid-ab-contraction, when his chin is tucked into his upper chest.

"Can you?" I ask.

"What, now?"

That night I try sleeping with my arm extended above my head. I prop it up with couch cushions and other pillows from around the house. I am fine for a while and then my arm begins to ache. I lie there staring at the ceiling and rubbing my finger against my lips. With my left arm, I reach over to Mickey and slip my hand beneath his pajamas, then his boxers.

"Now?" He looks over his shoulder at the pile of cushions. I tell him I can't sleep, it hurts too much.

"It's late," he says. It's a little after midnight.

"I know, I'm sorry." I move my hand down. He rolls over and tells me to get some sleep.

I am up at 5:30. I take six Aspirin and a shot of Tequila I hide behind the microwave; my finger is no better. At 7:30, I call in sick to work and get Debra.

"You still haven't gone to the hospital?" she says.

"I was waiting, I thought it would go down."

"Do you need a ride?" She sounds annoyed.

"No, of course not." I have to hang up because I'm in too much pain. I lie back on the couch and raise my arm over my head. I try to read magazines, but there are only *Men's Health* and *Health and Fitness*. When I wake up Mickey is squatting beside me, inspecting my finger.

"Did you take your B-12?" he asks.

"What?" I'm still coming out of sleep. "No, I forgot I guess." He is talking funny. I lower my arm slowly so it won't throb too much. Something shines from between his lips. I sit up fast.

"I think," he says standing up, "I should go in through the nail." A sewing needle sparkles on his tongue.

"Mickey," I say, "I want to go to the emergency room." He tips my head down and looks me in the eyes.

"You don't smell like liquor," he says, "do you?"

"What?" I say. He makes a show of looking me up and down, stopping at my feet in his new socks then at the mess of magazines on the floor.

"Are you drunk?"

"Jesus, I am not drunk." I push myself up out of the couch and slip on a magazine. "I'm going to the hospital," I say, walking past him to the bedroom. He grabs my shoulder and turns me around.

"You are not driving drunk." I realize my T-shirt is wet and clinging to my back. My forehead is damp. I could faint.

"Fine," I say. "I don't care, whatever, do it."

"Go sit, I'll get something for the blood." I follow him back into the kitchen and sit down at the table. He's beside me with a rag and a lighter. Under the lamplight, he holds the needle above the flame while the tip turns black. I am watching him for signs of pleasure as I remember it is my only needle.

"Is it going to feel better though?" I ask. He doesn't answer and he doesn't look up from the flame.

Turtle Hunting

TARA L. MASIH

He took me turtle hunting once. How many of you can say that your lovers have taken you turtle hunting?

We ask for sensitivity, but eventually their pain becomes more than we can bear.

I'll take you, he says. Maybe we'll find one.

And he pulls me through the trees, green-yellow dappling the spongy floor. We pause by granite slabs, tilted sideways to the earth, crimson ivy pulling them down. And we stand silently, our shadows falling over the dark stones.

We were intruders foreshadowing our own demise.

I try to read the chiseled names and dates eroded by lichen. Their names did not even last a century.

The turtles are by the water, he says. You can see their small nostrils sometimes, just above the surface.

We walk by the edge, and I try to share his wonder, try to ignore the swamp mud tugging at my white sneakers. I wipe them off on damp leaves of skunk cabbage when his back is turned. And I try not to mind the flame-colored poison ivy. I think of the turtles, their bodies sealed off from the world, breathing the only reason for them to stay in it.

They have survived millions of years, their reward for knowing the right balance between vulnerability and defense.

He gives up after a few hours, unsuccessful.

We want what does not exist.

What do you want to do now? Go home? he asks.

We return the way we thought we had come, but a sea of tall grass arrests our progress. Surrounded by grasshoppers, gossamer wings, he takes my hand.

This is the perfect place to make love, he says.

What must remain in order for us to be able to say that we have survived?

I turn my head, my sorrow one with the swarm of miniscule insects we slap away.

Call Carmine

BETH ANNE ROYER

Call Carmine and say dude, what are you doing showing up in my dreamlife 10 years late? You gave me nothing but a pile of rocks tucked into a little sack. What was that, Carmine? Call Carmine and ask him what's happening on his rooftop in Brooklyn. Is there a brunch this weekend? Call Carmine and ask him to call you by your old nickname, *tender buttons*. Say, Carm, please say it, *tender buttons*, say it just once. Are you alone Carm? Are you hungry? Tell him about the gazpacho you make these days, about how your cooking has improved since you dated in the 90s. Say, Carmine I'm no longer living on a diet of B.L.T.s. I can make a tasty spinach salad with mangos now. I have a good dog named Henrik. Say Carmine, what's new? Carmine, how are you, Carmine, what's been happening since I met up with you at that overpriced and underdelicious diner on West 7th in 1998? Say Carmine, I'm sorry I tried to kiss you when I knew you were dating that girl named Cande, but what kind of a name is Cande? Especially with an "e"? Call Carmine and ask him why his parents gave him such a wimpy-ass name. Call Carmine and ask if he still has your old letters and can you have them back? Call Carmine and hang up because his voice has become so adult you don't know who he is. Call Carmine. Call Carmine. Call Carmine.

Bouncing

KEITH LOREN CARTER

Standing at the kitchen sink, blinking away sleep, he hears his wife's scream "Oh God!" followed by a terrible bumping and crashing, which he knows as sure as he's standing there in his boxers is his baby son bouncing down the stairs, just as he has always feared, and he drops the coffee pot and runs to the foot of the staircase in time to catch the startled body as it tumbles off the last carpeted stair, a plastic toddler gate crashing behind and hitting—*Thock!*—the wall, leaving a big hole that could have easily been his son's perfect head, but instead he's holding that head in one hand, cradling the rest of his tense, Pooh-clad body in his arms, staring at the tiny face, contorted in a frozen, soundless scream of fear and wonder, smooth skin turning crimson, breath held for an eternity as he hears his wife's "Please God," echo his own prayers along with his voiced pleading "Breathe, Lorne," when the logjam breaks at last, tears flow and cries like someone is sticking him with a sewing needle erupt out of the suddenly heaving body, threatening to rupture his membranes, and then just as suddenly the cat strolls by, blissfully unconcerned with the drama before her, and the tortured expression of his son clears as sunny as a solstice morning, leaving only a mother and father, their lives no longer their own.

My Mother's Hair

DENISE DUHAMEL

My mother's "fall" on its Styrofoam head, the shiny chestnut *That Girl* flip that she wore out to dinner with her favorite perfume which came in a glass bottle with a tiger fur cap. I couldn't help but make little fingernail moons in the Styrofoam, whole eyebrows and lashes. The blank face scared me—it was the bumpy face of nightmares, monsters, people disappearing. I was glad when my mother put it away, into the shiny tube-shaped case that I used for my 45s after her "fall" went out of style.

She also had a two-foot blond braid that my sister wore with her gold beaded unitard for her modern jazz recital and I wore to a B-52's concert a few years later, swinging it around as I danced, afraid it might fall off and I'd lose it, the stunning synthetic snake.

My mother trusted her real hair to Roger, whose beauty parlor had an entrance in Massachusetts and an exit in Rhode Island. I'd run back and forth through both doors playing fugitive until he sat me down with his hardcover books of glamorous bouffants. I'd lose myself in the swirling curls of the models in the beauty parlor paintings with bamboo frames that hung over the chairs in his waiting room. My mother seemed so much smaller when her hair was wet. The hairdryers looked like astronaut helmets. I was mesmerized by the black combs that bobbed in aqua Barbercide.

Since her accident, my mother goes to a new stylist before she's technically open. She jokes with my mother—*your scars don't bother me, I work part time for a funeral parlor.* I miss my mother's hair—her fake hair, her real hair, her teased hair, her perms. My mother gives me her headbands and bobbie pins, saying, *I won't be using these anymore.* I miss my mother's hair paraphernalia—the rinses, the rollers, the AquaNet, the pin curls, the clear rain bonnet that folded into what looked like a tiny suitcase and disappeared.

A Med School Lesson

R. S. STEINBERG

The neurologists sent me and Fleckman to work up a hairy two hundred pound adolescent in a giant crib with a tennis net over the top. Wee Fleckman in his paisley bow tie and German horn rims was first in our class. They picked me because I played rugby.

The brain condition made Donny violent. "Careful," Fleckman said. Donny grunted and bit Fleckman's stethoscope. Fleckman tugged. Donny ripped the sleeve off his white coat. I tightened the tennis net. Fleckman went to change.

The neurologists recommended an EEG. Fleckman wrote the requisition. I helped wheel the crib. Donny hurled himself at the aide and screeched in the elevator. When they put needles in Donny's scalp he decked the technician and trashed the lab.

Fleckman brought me a syringe of paraldehyde, an acrid-smelling sedative mixed in mineral oil. "Give this to him rectally."

"If you hold him."

The technicians hunkered down behind the turned-over crib. Fleckman cringed and said I should hold Donny and he'd give it. Hairy Donny farted. I wrestled him down. Fleckman stuck the rubber tube in. Donny relaxed and smiled. "See?" said Fleckman, and pushed the paraldehyde.

"Bye-bye," Donny said, and expelled oily paraldehyde and worse all over Fleckman. Then he went to sleep.

The EEG was important and interesting. Fleckman changed into a perfect white coat to present it at grand rounds, where the chief neurologist who complimented his skillful management of the difficult patient told me I could learn much from Fleckman.

How To Become a Country-Western Singer

LEE HARRINGTON

First your girlfriend has to move out, taking everything from the Lovett albums to the leftover beans-and-franks. Then you rush to your secret letter drawer; sure enough, the latest from Dolly-Sue are missing. Minutes later, snow begins to fall. Ice collects on the gutters and eaves. At midnight, black water seeps through the ceiling and onto your white shag rug. Your girlfriend calls while you're on your knees, positioning pots and pans beneath the drips. "You cheat too much," she says. "You're lazy and selfish and you never make me laugh."

You stand and cough and tell her marriage could change all that.

"Well, what about those goddamn extension cords?" she says.

"Extension cords?"

On the radio, DJ Charles Francis says something about the coldest winter in forty years.

"Can't you string them behind furniture like normal people?" she says. "Not straight across the floor?" She screams something about land-mines and subconscious sabotage and slams down the phone.

You step over a few of these cords: bass-amp, floor lamp, mike. Apparently they represent some major character flaw. You try to read them like life-lines on a palm. *Like life-lines on a palm!*

There's a song in this, you tell yourself, and open a bottle of rum. You sit on the rug and listen; if you listen, the music will come.

The popcorn bowl clacks and the mini-wok thwacks. The ice

in your glass makes a tinkly-wind-chime sound. But the rhythm needs work. You'll try less ice, more rum. Then you'll add some pathetic lyrics. Later, when the bottle's empty, you can lie among the extension cords and compare the sound of water hitting skin. Maybe it will thud like a broken heart.

DANCING

MARIETTE LANDRY

I haven't mastered the wedding steps: Fox Trot, Tarantella, Waltz. But I'm watching women my mother's age follow their partners without effort, eyes up, smiling, making small talk with others just like them. These are women who've learned. They've developed a sixth sense for sudden changes of direction, or heart, who move as if their own feet were attached, the same way they practiced as girls, like this, dancing on their fathers' shoes.

I'm seated at the Table of the Unattached: boy, girl, boy, girl. "You want to give it a whirl?" the guy beside me asks. The answer is no, but he's up already, and he's got me by the wrist, and before I know it we're on the dance floor without license, frauds among the pros, and I can't follow, and he can't lead, so we bump backs with experts and trip on each other's toes. He's awkward, I'm depressed, and my friend, the bride, has just married the wrong guy. I scan the room for an open door. I have the urge to run. "Dip me," I say instead. He hesitates. "Will you just do it!"

An elderly couple helps me up off my ass. The man offers balance by way of a firm hold at my elbow, and the wife doesn't say what she thinks: *This one's had a few too many*. And I understand, suddenly, how pointless it would be to set her straight. What sense could she make of a modern woman, sober, who gets what she asks for?

LOVE AND MURDER

RUSTY BARNES

Katherine waited as Gallow puttered with the tackle box in the bed of the truck. He always took so long about things. She heard a vague noise, some music, start up from one of the nicer picnic grounds on the hill above them, but she didn't listen to music anymore other than what Gallow played on his guitar. It was one of the prices you paid for marriage, losing part of yourself, your music. She'd noticed this, and other things, as soon as she started in with Brady Bragg.

"I brought along some stuff to keep you company." Gallow wagged a newly burned CD at her, then thrust it into the truck's player. It took a moment to reach her, a crawling and skittery rockabilly riff that the truck's sound system rattled all the way across the water. Someone would be calling the park rangers in about it, no doubt, but they would be on the lake already. The rangers would just reach into the truck and turn it off. She watched Gallow in his cutoff jeans as he lumbered down the boat ramp and into the hip-high water. She held the boat with an oar to the bottom against the slight current. "Shit. You didn't have to let it drift so far," Gallow said. He got in smoothly, but the boat dipped under his weight, became unsteady.

"I didn't. The boat's right where you told me to keep it. It just moved a little." She planted the oar more firmly. Brady was somewhere here too, she knew. They'd planned it loosely, that Gallow would get preoccupied with fishing, that she would get hot, feel faint, and have to go back in, where Brady would be waiting. Already she could almost feel Brady watching her from somewhere in the pines along the shore, wondering how much longer it would be before she'd force Gallow to take her back in, and that knowledge was a cold thing she kept in her heart for when she would need it.

Gallow pulled at the oars and took them to the far side of the lake, into the shade where he said the bass were. Katherine didn't know if that was true or not—how could he know where the fish were?—but she knew the sun on his bulky shoulders had to be punishing him, so shade made sense. While she felt badly for him, it didn't seem to matter that within a half hour or so, she would be messing with Brady Bragg somewhere in those cooler woods. She and Gallow had been through it all, the permutations of what will you do for me, why can't you do this, will you change this, this isn't how it's supposed to be, and they seemed to agree to this uneasy equilibrium in which he would ask no questions of her and in return she would go on taking care of Ricky and Meurine and Josette. She periodically opened her legs and let him fumble between them in his well-meaning way. She pretended to smile when he wrote love songs for her on that long beaten-up guitar. But Gallow's love for her now was a virus she hoped she wouldn't catch and return, the way common illnesses like colds and love spread.

Gallow shipped the oars and let the boat drift, waves lapping at the sides now in a parody of tranquility, and all she could think of was Brady rocking into her as he pinned her hands over her head. Gallow picked his pole up and grinned at her, cast his line into the water and waited for a bite. Gallow would never pin her, imply violence in any way—he was too kind by far—and it had been something she immediately felt as a need that might be difficult to express to him, though in his way, he might have tried for her, which would have made the point moot, the fantasy unreal. Nor did she want to explain this to Gallow, so it made a sort of futile, tiring sense that the thing she might feel most comfortable getting from someone she trusted, she got from someone she was unsure of. Maybe that was part of the thrill too. Not only was it an affair, this thing with Brady, Katherine told herself, it was passionate and maybe violent, like waves crashing or something, like a romance novel, except real.

She reached a decision quickly, stood and dove into the water, into the cool depths to the limit of her lungs, then arched her body like a boomerang and shot herself back toward the air, where she broke the surface to Gallow swearing. "Kate," he said. "I mean, what the fuck?"

"I'm hot. This fucking trip was your idea." She moved her hair from her eyes while treading water.

"I wanted to spend time with you."

"Fish, Gallow. Go catch something, anything. I'm going in to take a nap now that I'm cooled off." Katherine started the swim to the shore in a quick crawl, not waiting to hear what he said, nor caring. When she reached the shore and sloshed her way up the boat ramp, picking at her clinging shorts, Brady was already there at the truck, waiting for her. She looked back quickly over her shoulder, where Gallow, as always, would do what she'd told him to—let her cool out, he would think—and fish, mull over whatever it was he could imagine he had done to deserve this. He was a pale dot now on the larger green of the lake, casting toward the shore over and over, as if his line wouldn't play.

"Mmmm," Brady said, as he reached into Gallow's truck and turned off the music. He put his face between her breasts and licked. "Cocoa butter and fish-shit. Fucking-A."

"Brady. Don't talk." Katherine took him by the hands, walked to the back of the truck and helped him in, bringing him to her. She could hear the tick of the steel in the truck bed, and as she lay there with Brady she imagined Gallow coming back to discover them; it would be a murder, maybe, as if in a movie, the crunch of footsteps in the gravel, the adrenal rush. She imagined all the gory details even as Brady pinned her wrists to the spare tire and pushed into her; she closed her eyes against the thoughts, shifted under him, a bolt pushing into her lower back. Brady grunted, whispered something guttural into her ear, and against her will she thought of Gallow fishing now in the middle of the lake, all that dark green water around him, and of the sound love might make if it were like the water pushing against the boat, ceaseless, forever.

ALFALFA

TERRY THUEMLING

The fight started with a simple cryptogram in the Sunday edition of *The New York Times: Find a word with the letter combination XYZXYZX,* but things escalated, as they inevitably do, and soon it was no longer a friendly contest to see who could solve the puzzle first but a battle fought tooth and nail across a glass coffee table, the outcome of which would be the surest sign yet of who was smarter, thus settling a furtive rivalry that loomed over their new marriage like a cartoon anvil and had recently intensified thanks to comments such as, *Oh come on, my twelve-year-old niece knows Bismarck is the capital of North Dakota, Thirty-five across is harebrained, not "hairbrained," and Well sure, I used to think existentialism was interesting too, but that was back in high school,* and even though they were both educated and believed themselves to be above the things about which most newlyweds bickered, they still found themselves arguing over equally trivial matters—the significance of SAT scores, who had actually read Baudelaire in French, or the proper pronunciation of Nabokov—at the same time they both knew these subjects had little to do with the questions they really wanted to ask, the answers they wanted to hear, so then there they were in the middle of a row over a word game, saying nasty things about each other's parents and threatening to give up on the whole *damn* marriage, emphasizing each point by pounding the tabletop when suddenly the glass surface shattered into a thousand tiny pieces and they were left wondering what just happened, until one of them figured it out.

PHOTO BY THE BED

JENNIFER CARR

Your mother hands me photos from your childhood like a test. "Which one is Alec?" she says, tapping the edge. I study the faces of you and your twin, both round, both framed with dark hair, eyes squinted with smile. Your face is almost wider, your nose not quite as long, but what clues me in is that you're always leaning forward. You're the one reaching for the camera, or ready to jump from the frame. You have three minutes and forty-five seconds of seniority on this earth, and you knew it even then. I pick you successfully and the day continues, Easter or birthday, the day continues.

When she visits, she picks up the frame on the nightstand. In the picture, your father is laughing. A beard, John Lennon glasses, a bandana pushing back his hair, then dark. He is a man with two young boys, a man that does not yet know the pain of his wife's affair, the pain of growing to be the father of only a house. His own parents will be dead in two years. He is the age we are now.

In the picture, you stand with your twin in front, five years old. You're both wearing those striped railroad caps we all wore—I was wearing too, five hundred miles and seventeen years away. She hands me the picture, and this is no test, this is the photo by the bed. I point to you and your mother shakes her head, points to your brother. You nod in confirmation. "No," I tell her, then immediately quiet, frightened I've been loving the wrong face, searching the wrong face, searching the one in the white shirt these years for signs of you.

458 Miles Through the Texas Panhandle with the Former Love of my Life

JEN HELLER

When we reach Sweetwater, it's your turn to drive. I stretch out in the back seat, and for eleven towns I try to fall asleep. I shift positions, crunching bags of pretzels with my feet; my reckless kicks send empty Coke cans rolling. I even try to sleep sitting up Indian style, but it's no use. I rescue one of your stupid guitar magazines from between the seat cushions and flip through it until I feel carsick.

In Coleman we stop for gas and the store cashier, a bony Barbara Mandrell-type, warns us about the storm. "There's a nasty tornado headed west," she says. "If you keep going east, you'll hit it head on." She traces the countertop with two pointed fingers and mashes their tips together, causing a devastating imaginary collision.

Near Lampasas we see it, wide and red as an open mouth. I press my forehead to the window and fog the glass with warm worried breath. But you, you're blank all over, eyes straight ahead, and I want to crawl inside your calmness – crack it open and act as if nothing has happened, like the wind that just minutes away is peeling bricks from houses. "We're in Travis County," you announce proudly at dusk, but my noise makes your voice too small to be heard. I am amorphous, fast spinning, destructive. "Remorseless," you tell reporters later at the scene of our disaster, and they can see that you are horrified.

How To Cheat (On Your Wife)

LATANYA MCQUEEN

It's on the left. The sign in front says "Peep shows after eight, Vids two for one." Parking's in the rear because it's on the side of the highway and not everyone in town needs to know your business. Once inside, skip past the dildos, bigger than you could've imagined, past the kink games, the novelty items. Head to the back where the tapes are, you know the ones, that's where you need to go. Your eyes will roam past hardcore, voyeur, lesbian, bondage . . . Grab a video, maybe one from the bargain half-off bin. Find the cheapest one because you're not picky, not now.

Pay in cash, give the man at the front the crumpled twenty you've had in your hand, damp from palm's sweat. He'll put down the bean burrito wrapped in foil on the counter. Ignore his comments about the choice you made as his greasy fingers take the money. The change, take the change, you'll need it soon. Go back to your car, the Honda minivan your wife made you buy, smiling as she rubbed her fingers along the back of your neck and whispered "an investment for the future." You jerk off in the backseat, watching the screen up above, to some girl with lips the color of cherries shouting "oh yes, oh yes, oh . . ."

Pick up milk at the gas station, remember that's what you left for, and go home. Your wife's in the kitchen wearing one of your dirty t-shirts, stirring beef stew in a pot and dancing to a pop song on the radio. Watch her as she tries to move, missing beats, sweating from steam. You can't help yourself, still hearing the moans of someone else. You make love to her there on the kitchen linoleum, all sparkle and shine, forgetting the stew until it boils over, making stains on the stove she'll have to scrub. Then later like rabbits you're at it again in the bathroom, her fingers claw into your shoulders as your eyes focus on the flowered wallpaper, peeling. When it's over she apologizes for the gashes, goes back to stirring stew, and asks if you got milk, but you're already gone.

Braggo Roth's Bag o' Broth

BRAIIAN RUUSKA

Who knows what became of him after leaving the majors in 1921, but I believe Braggo Roth missed a swell opportunity for wealth and fame by refusing to associate himself with a product my grandfather proposed: Braggo Roth's Bag o' Broth. Grandpa Joe was buried with the final letter Roth sent him: "Foolhardy!" it simply declared.

My grandfather has long since left this earth, and with him the knowledge of how the Bag o' Broth was to function, but according to my grandmother, it appeared to be nothing more than a plain brown paper bag. But when you'd put it to your mouth and inhale, your insides would be filled with a warming, flavorful broth. You could even fold it up and carry it in your pocket for days at a time. I don't know how it was heated or how the broth got into the bag, and I fear I'll never know, but it's an invention that would have been invaluable during the Depression and wars that followed Roth's retirement. Tragically, his letter drove my grandfather to destroy the prototype in frustration, and within days he contracted the brain fever that was to claim his life.

Braggo Roth played for six teams over eight seasons, compiling a robust .284 batting average. He was a solid outfielder, but not one that should be enshrined at Cooperstown. Every day he becomes more and more obscure in our memory. It seems to me that his only reasons for being were to provide a few timely base hits and to inspire a young man in Athol, Massachusetts, listening to the Sox on the radio. But instead Roth's lack of faith or imagination doomed our family; like my father before me, I spend my nights in a basement laboratory, trying to stumble upon Grandpa Joe's secret. To date, my best effort has been the Carpet o' Broth, which, while remarkable, is completely impractical. I fear that I too will fail, and that one day my son will discover my journals and attempt to continue my life's futile work. I ought to burn those notebooks now, while my faculties are still intact, but how can I be sure the answer isn't somewhere in those pages?

Memoir of a Bookshelf

LESLIE BUSLER

Sarah, Plain and Tall • Are You There God, It's Me Margaret • What's Happening to My Body? • Boy Meets Girl • What I Know Now • Go Ask Alice • Other Voices, Other Rooms • Sense and Sensibility • Breakfast at Tiffany's • Ain't I a Beauty Queen? • The Heart of the Matter • Heart Songs and Other Stories • The Heart Is a Lonely Hunter • Heart of Darkness • Death of the Heart • A Farewell to Arms • Mrs. Dalloway • The Feminine Mystique • The Bell Jar • The Bullfighter Checks Her Makeup • Theatre of the Oppressed • Our Bodies, Ourselves • Lolita • The Holy Bible • Spirituality at Work • The Devil: A Biography • Ordinary People as Monks and Mystics • The Meditative Mind • Yoga: Moving Into Stillness • The Kama Sutra • Women on Top: How Real Life Has Changed Women's Fantasies • You Don't Say: Modern American Inhibitions • The Joy of Sex • How to be Good • Bridget Jones' Diary • Pride and Prejudice • All About Love: New Visions • Catch-22 • The Headless Cupid • Curses, Hexes, and Spells • Celibacy Is Better than Really Bad Sex • How to Lose Friends and Alienate People • One Hundred Years of Solitude • Darkness Visible • How to Save Your Own Life • The Sun Also Rises • The Book of Laughter and Forgetting

TRAIN-JUMPING

ASHLEY RICE

We were living outside a junction town just north of the Blue Ridge Mountains. Each night when the trains came through they rattled the panes of my bedroom window. I couldn't sleep so I'd count the stars stuck on my ceiling. Momma would be in the front room arguing with Daddy, the television up loud, trying to connect with the rest of America.

Each night, I counted the plastic stars until they were just numbers in my head. Then one night when I was supposed to be asleep I spotted a deer standing still and poised outside my window. That deer stood there a second on just three legs very poised and when it sensed a train approaching from around the bend, that deer, it started running.

However: "Cheryl Ann, don't go out by the woods at night," Daddy had warned me. "You know what can happen by the woods at night."

With the rains came the chiggers thick as June itself. Then Daddy lost his job, the rains stopped too completely and a major power plant closed down. By mid-summer, the house was stifling. Already, from the heat I had bad hives. The first night, I put on shorts and a gray short-sleeved shirt, and—ignoring the gray roar of the television set—from my opened back-window, I climbed outside.

Within a few minutes, my itching was gone because of a strong, metallic breeze arriving as a train itself came roaring by. Those trains ran so close to our old house—right through our fenceless backyard, practically—but they ran far too fast right there for anyone to ever catch them. And everyone knew that if a train was not slowed down enough, and you tried to catch a hold of it, you'd slide under the tracks and immediately be gone, sort of like drowning.

But off to the left, behind Mrs. Smith's house, was a crossing-over-place by a bridge and also by a water tower where each and every train slowed down. We were lucky we had such a slow-down-place because it was the single and only one left in our entire county.

So that night, when I spotted the train nearing that flat, hardened slow place, I hit the ground and ran for the woods where the tracks were as fast as I could. And then when I saw the old reddened boxcars slowing just for me, I ran even faster: the row of telephone poles to the left, not beside me, the train right out in front of me, the pinpricked sky at a tilt, and then I just jumped. Caught a hold of a handle—pulled myself up.

Then: the trees rushing by. All those trees rushing by.

It was the simplest night jump, right then, of risking everything to catch a hold of them. That summer did not let up, and I rode that same line twenty-three times. Each time I'd close my eyes, count out a slow ten, and then I would leap off. Near the post office was a soft place where I'd jump out and roll, then run home through the woods, knowing that, in hitting the right mossy spot just before the rocks began, and the drop-offs began, just how very lucky I was.

Being a crop carrier, that train did not slow again for three more long state lines. A neighbor kid fell asleep and woke up out in the land of California. Another little neighbor boy lost his only left leg forever. Course my own Daddy caught me running full-out down towards those glinting tracks one moonshine and moonlit night and paddled me good.

Then we moved away from the house with the stars on the ceiling. We moved to a town with white dam water churning,

churning. A school bus town. A mining hideaway town (used-to-be).

And then kept going.

Oral Fixations

LEE HARRINGTON

As a baby I was addicted to pacifiers. They say that will happen if you're not breast-fed.

I sucked my thumb until I was twelve. The orthodontist detected an overbite, and Mother had to douse my thumb with Tabasco sauce every night until I was cured.

When my hair was long enough I sucked on that. I always wore two braids—one in each corner of my mouth, like a bridle.

After the pixie cut, I chewed pencils, cracking the yellow paint with my teeth. I read somewhere you could get lead poisoning; I stopped.

I chewed bubble gum through Middle School. If the flavor ran out, I got irritable, and couldn't concentrate unless I kept a tough, fruity wad—four or five pieces—in my mouth. The dentist found 16 cavities.

In high school it was cigarettes. We stole them from our mothers—Virginia Slims from Mrs. Olsen, Kent Golden Lights from Mrs. Tall. We stood in circles in the woods and passed them around, each of us taking thoughtful drags.

These days I kiss boys. Boys are everywhere on campus, and each one tastes different. One will taste fresh, like cinnamon; the next may taste foul, like onions on a sub. It's impossible to stop.

786 WORDS

AN ACCOUNT OF THE LIFE OF DOCTOR VICTOR FRANKENSTEIN

CAM TERWILLIGER

There in the Academy chamber, which was more like a kitchen than anything, his only guests were the piles of bodies, which lined the halls of the vault. A coroner by trade, it was his job to catalogue their thumbs and ears, arms and legs, stomachs, tongues, and brains. The eyes, of course, were a personal favorite. He loved their colored rings: the festive speckled green of the iris, the unpolluted black of the pupil. Wherever he went he carried with him a long felt-lined case, brimming with calipers, and more calipers. Needless to say, he took the dimensions of everything.

He was good. He knew that much. How to separate flesh from bone, dissolve it, petrify it. How to squeeze the alcoholic liver through the mouth of a Mason jar. He knew everything—all the Moorish techniques, how to unlock the cage of the ribs. A master of phrenology, he groped their skulls, reading the Braille of follicles and the divisions where bone meets bone. The dead would dance for him, cropping their innards to the sky and begging, "me next, me next." But when he paused, they paused. And, at end of the day, when he stopped, they stopped. Without him, they could only lie slack on the floor like a procession of unstrung puppets.

It was sad, the way he went on like this, trying to balance the account of their lives—as if explaining might do anyone any good now. What bothered him most were the scars. There was no end to what life might etch on their still living skins, tearing it like paper, or a thin coat of wax. There was so much mutilation. Only yesterday, he had discovered a man clubbed to death by his own wooden leg. Things like that were the worst. The things they did to each other. And the things they did to themselves.

Then, one day, after entering 12 more love-related suicides, he made his decision. He would make a creature of his own—a perfectly formed little man with ears like water chestnuts, and hair one shade darker than corn silk. Something that could eat a grapefruit, he thought. Something that could sit at the hearth, warming its feet by the fire. It would stay hidden with him, there underground, where its bones could never be broken, its inability to swim could never be mocked. Instead, he would teach it things, such as Chaucer and the correct pronunciation of Latin. On its twelfth birthday, he would give it a harmonica.

Beneath his giant copper vat, he shoveled a mound of smoking coal. He stoked it to 98.6 degrees, then added a solution of water, ashes, and dust. With an oar, he began to stir the rest in: kidneys, lungs, eyes, a luxurious scalp of strawberry blonde. He knew all the ratios exactly. Adrenaline, starch, blood, bile, green and black phlegm. One third fibrous muscle. One quarter fat. A powerful, burgundy heart, still beating from the ox. A cabbage shaped brain (medium wrinkled) and, lastly, a bucket of 206 beautiful, ivory bones.

But in the morning, when he pried the lid off, the one thing that arose was an unbearable, sulfurous stink. No little man. No water chestnuts. So he tried it again, this time waiting nine months. But still, it failed; so he began to alter the recipe. Yeast, he added, along with his memories chiseled into a tablet. He tried adding more fire, less water. He tried kites. He tried straining a pint of seal blubber. He added a three-piece suit, then a two-piece, both of them pinstriped. He tried counting the number of cells. He tried combinations of gold, and of horse manure. He even dripped beads of his own glistening sweat from the end of a rolling pin. He removed a rib. He added an extra. He stood watch for 48 hours, reading the Koran and the Gospels, hoping, hoping that words might sow the floating bits of flesh together. He added volumes of history, a wooden marionette, seven kinds of apples and, of course, there were his bottles and bottles of sorrow.

Nothing worked. And so, he had to pack up the vault and retire.

At the end, all he wanted to know was "How?" How, despite all the moaning, the injuries, the misshapen limbs, and the teeth, which are always falling out, did people go on? There must be some hidden ingredient. A thread bound to the base of the spine like a coiled snake. Or perhaps, a pebble nestled in the pit of the chest that tells them: you must continue, go on my sons and daughters, go on, limping together, shambling after the sun.

At the Movies

CHRISTOPHER HELMUTH

I'm in the mood for Action/Adventure when we arrive at the Cineplex, but Donna says she'll make it worth my while if we see the movie of my life, so that's what we see. Even though it's the Friday after Thanksgiving, we're the only ones in our theater except an old couple with matching red sweaters and a large middle-aged woman reading a magazine.

The opening scenes are nice enough: my first smile, my first word, my first steps, my first bike. Donna pats my cheek and grins. I score the winning goal, I win the spelling bee, I pummel bully Chris Newman on the bus. Donna cheers, feels my biceps. Soon her hand moves down to my thigh.

Then I'm twelve, jerking off in the closet. Donna takes her hand away. I hear distant screams for help, and there's this close-up of my eyes looking up, but I only pause for a moment before I keep going. Afterward, I'm in the kitchen getting a glass of milk, and I see flames coming from the neighbors' roof and people leaning over lifeless bodies. I hear sirens. I go back to my room and swear to God I'll never lust again. This promise isn't enough for the old couple, who scowl at us as they leave.

I hope I'll be shown playing checkers with my grandfather or maybe we'll see a montage of me dropping money into offering plates and Salvation Army buckets, but naturally the next scene opens with a porno and pans back to me sitting between empty bottles and soccer buddies. Jackson and I are barely conscious, but Thompson recommends we egg cars from the bridge over the turnpike, so all seven of us pile into Walker's Oldsmobile. On the way, Walker suggests we trip on the butane in our lighters. He and Thompson howl out the windows, Curtis and I wonder how much a hooker costs and if we have enough cash between us, and everyone takes a sniff. When we get back to the house, Jackson's out cold. In fact, he's blue and isn't breathing. We take him to the hospital, dump him on the lawn, honk three times, and take off as the shot dissolves.

In the next scene I score another winning goal, and all of us celebrate, but then a camera zooms in on my black armband.

Donna stands and puts on her coat after the sex scene involving one of my students. I tell her that it gets better, that soon he meets this beautiful, patient, compassionate woman at a Labor Day picnic and falls madly in love. After she comes along, I say, he's a new man. I tell her I know it will have a happy ending.

But of course it ends predictably.

I Always Know It's Over When They Say:

MELISSA MCCRACKEN

You never met a man like me before. My wife has nothing to do with this. You remind me of my mother. I want seven children. I have three kids. I'll never get over her. My ex wouldn't swallow. Lemme buy you a drink. I only drink when I'm depressed. My British accent only comes out when I'm drunk, Love. Last time, I wrecked the El Camino. I only bet on college ball. I haven't finished a book since high school. I quit the hard drugs. I can't wait until deer season.

Broads. Dames. Kiddo. Cunt.

I like you just the way you are, but you'd be a knockout if you lost 15 pounds. Flowers just die anyway. How many men have you slept with? You like women? I hate cats. I hate condoms. The Beatles suck. I'm still planning on getting my GED. I'm a lawyer. I'm a gynecologist. I vote pro-life. Don't call me here. Call me in the car. I'll call my secretary and have her make reservations. She deserved it. I have a jealous streak. You're cute when you're angry. Where's your sense of humor? Wanna fuck? I have a Polaroid.

I can't smile without you. I can't take my eyes off of you. I'll be watching you. I love you.

Death Angels

RUSTY BARNES

Mathis. *Amanita Virosa* springs from the soil after days of heavy rain. You have to be careful your dog doesn't eat it. You have to be careful your kids don't eat it. It's very tempting, this lily-white shroom with a dark underside. It will kill you dead, and thus you may want to have a party, an after-rain soirée that includes close examination of the ground, just for this purpose, and you should invite all the people in the world that you hate.

Mathis, your death angels are springing forth from the ground even as we speak. The rain falls from the sky, travels in runnels down the leaves of the huge spreading oak in your yard, drops onto the acidic soil, and grows. Overnight it will become as big as a garden rock, but right now it is a tiny fillip of fiber, so small you will need a flashlight and tweezers to find it. Your wife says the same thing about you when she yaks with her friends. She is the first person you invite.

The second person you invite is Matty, your best friend, your wife's lover. You imagine that Matty and Mathis are close enough in the ear-breathy sex-syllabics that when your wife moans in pleasure under one or the other of you, whatever name she mutters is okay by whomever.

Matty likes cars and psilocybin and women, not necessarily in that order, so he is unpleasantly tight when he arrives late, pupils dilated—dreamy and fulsome and annoying—chattering in his Carlos-Castaneda-used-car-salesman way about his '69 Camaro. It shines redly in the slick of water pouring from the sky. Matty goes over and takes your wife by the elbow and leads her to the corner of your deck, where the rain drips down onto her neck. She squeals all girly-like and you wish you had two of her to introduce to more friends, so that they all could know how good you have it.

The third person you invite is your mother, and the last your father, so as to get the Oedipals out of the way.

Three is a magic number, says the children's ditty. You've included one to grow on.

Death is not the end, Mathis, but it's a good start, you think, and it is time now to search the lawn for these puffballs of doom, these little white shrooms, and you are on your knees in the deep wet of your unmowed lawn, the smell of grass and dirt in your nostrils, and your own fate in the trowel you hold, digging.

Green Grass
A Fable

JENNIFER CARR

Once upon a time, there was a man who married a beautiful woman and they had a house with a road that stretched out before them looking so much like life. On the other side of the road, the grass was greener, but maybe it was because the man who owned it was a farmer, and in any event, the man with the beautiful wife thought the farmer a cranky neighbor. So he looked down the road.

Down the road was a fat woman with heavy mascara and swells of perfume who sat behind the clipped hedge of her driveway, waiting for handsome married men to walk by. One day she saw the man walk slowly past her yard, absent the little blonde woman she sometimes saw with him at Star Market.

"Marry me!" she hissed from the hedge. She was a fat woman, and when she said these words, they swished around in her cheeks before she let them see air, so when they came out, they sounded like the hushed whisper of someone's love.

"I can't marry you," said the man. "I am already married." The man paused by the neatly paved driveway leading up to the dark brick ranch.

"Love me!" the woman said. "Let your children call me 'Mom'!" The woman was a fat woman, but only because she'd swallowed so much hope, and so many little bugs as she mowed her lawn each week in nice flat rows to make it green, green, green.

"Woman!" the woman's husband yelled from the screen door of the ranch house. "Make me dinner!" The woman's husband was not an evil man, just overtired from working a long day delivering Coca Cola to major universities in the area.

When the woman stood to go inside, the man noticed a strand of faux pearls dribbling into her cleavage, and that the gold-colored vest she wore was tight around her flowering chest. The man saw that the woman was bursting with life, desire, hope. The man was still young then, the age of his children now, and he thought life was just one big thing that stretched down a road.

That night, the man went home to his beautiful wife. "I'm going to do something but I'm not going to tell you what because it will make you very sad," he told her.

"Oh! I don't want to be sad!" the beautiful wife said.

"So I won't tell you," the man said. "And, anyhow, if I don't tell you, I won't feel as guilty over what I'm about to do. I will tell you, my beautiful wife, that I am working late."

"Oh!" the wife said. "I hurt already! Here are your two babies. They will miss you, too."

The man looked at his two babies: boy, girl—girl, boy—the same selection as he could find anywhere. And besides, they seemed so skinny, so drained of desire and zest for life, that he wanted, for a moment, to put cotton in their cheeks to make them look cherubic. Instead, he said to his beautiful wife, "I must go now. I have to work."

"Why?" she said as he walked down the drive. The wife was a beautiful wife, with long blonde hair and pure hazel eyes. But as she watched her husband walk toward the road, she wanted very much not to hurt, to cinch the ache she felt rising in her chest. She swallowed a breath of air then, and held it tightly in her throat until she felt the ache subside, dissolve.

"Why?" she said again. "Why walk to work? Take the Honda."

And so the man worked for many years, and his children grew up, as he knew they would, but had barely believed. "Why are you always working?" they asked.

"I want to give you everything," the man told them. They

were the age he had once been, when he first saw the road. "I want you to have everything I did not have." It was true. He did work hard, he did want many things for them. He also wanted, very much, for them to believe in him and his beautiful wife, the strong power of two people, raising two more. He sent them to universities of their choice, bought them both cars, and he and his blonde wife (now dyed) waved from the front door as the children backed out of the drive.

A long time ago, once, he hit her. (This is not the nice part of the fable; this is the brick oven, the wolf's teeth.) The children were young when it happened, though they did not understand, then. But it was a long time ago, once.

Years later it came time for the daughter to have coffee with her father. She did not want to be adult when he told her, she wanted to slap her hands on the table and scream *This Sucks!* but she kept her hands at her side because she was learning things though she didn't want to. He told her that sometimes the fat lady from the hedge phoned at three in the morning and woke the beautiful wife, who now ate pastries, and full dinners with second helpings, and now had a body large enough to contain her dormant hope.

The story didn't end because the daughter couldn't find the moral. Besides, Christmas was coming up, then Easter and so on.

"I love you," the man told his daughter. "This is so hard."

Because the moral has yet to be found, the story hasn't ended, but can take one of three paths:

1. The man shacks up with the fat lady from the hedge. The week he makes the move, he learns his beautiful wife signed up for lawn lessons, and now he's doomed to drive past the green green grass that used to be his own.

2. The man goes back to the beautiful wife and confesses. She acts shocked and enraged though the truth is less than she sus-

pected. She even cries a little bit, and walks away from the exchange with a mink, a diamond, a set of Calphalon pans, and the game point for every future argument.

3. Nothing happens. How could it? Of course the man goes back to his wife, of course they try to patch things up. The wife does cry, she is shocked, and the man knows that this is the hairline fracture, the eggshell on which he must walk. Somewhere in this time he realizes that life is calculated in years and he's used half his up.

SUDDEN, FLASH, QUICK: AN AFTERWORD

PAMELA PAINTER

Short shorts have long been a part of the literary landscape, but the eighties and nineties brought a renewed energy to the form and magazines began devoting sections or issues to the short short story. The *North American Review* was one of the first magazines to regularly publish what they called "Four-Minute Fictions," which editor Robley Wilson eventually collected in *Four-Minute Fictions: 50 short short stories from the North American Review* in 1987. In the nineties, Emerson College became a leading school for the development of the short short story, with our students at the leading edge of a genre that is gaining even more attention among writers.

On my desk at Emerson, I have a photograph of an orange crate. The actual orange crate has pictures of oranges pasted on it—a collage put together by a former student, Brian Hinshaw, in lieu of the crate of oranges that was his award for placing first in *The World's Best Short Short Story Contest*. Brian's story "The Custodian" occupied the position of honor on the broadside sent to all entrants, and though no oranges ever appeared at Brian's door, Jerome Stern's annual contest brought enormous focus to the short short story form. Eventually, many of the stories he and his judges selected as finalists for his contest or printed in *Sun Dog: The Southeast Review*, were collected in his superb tiny anthology, *Micro Fiction*, published by W.W. Norton, which includes the work of four Emerson students.

Brian Hinshaw was in one of my first short short story graduate workshops—a class I began teaching in the early nineties when workshops at most writing programs were still labeled "fiction" and "poetry," with no subtitles such as "linked stories" or "the first novel." After writing several short shorts in my regular fiction workshop, students successfully circulated a petition asking Emerson to allow one of my classes to be a workshop that focused solely on the short short story form. This was the beginning of Emerson's strong engagement with and support for the short short. The class started the next fall and for that semester, twelve students wrote a new short short story every week.

Over the years I've made a number of changes and additions to the story-a-week structure. After the first workshop, instead of saying "OK, next week bring in another story," I began to give students a subject or suggested form, which made writing a new story every week easier. Each class, I came up with a new exercise, such as "Write a 'How to...' story." Lee Harrington's "How to be a Country Western Singer" and Stace Budzko's "How to Set a House on Fire" were responses to this exercise.

Most of the writers in this collection were in one of my short-short classes and much of this work was born from these exercises. Amanda Holzer and Chip Cheek wrote their stories in response to the "write a list" exercise. Molly Lanzarotta and Joanne Avallon wrote dramatic "one-sentence" stories. Terry Thuemling and Derrick Ableman wrote their stories about playing a game. Matt Marinovich wrote a story to include: "a young narrator whose father is in jail." Heather Quarles borrowed Baby Bear from "Goldilocks and the Three Bears" for the exercise about "borrowing characters."

Ron Carlson's exercise "Solving for X" gave form to the stories of Ashley Rice and Leslie Busler. In this exercise, the first word of the first sentence begins with A, the first word of the second sentence begins with B, and the first word of the last sentence begins with Z. There are twenty-six sentences in the story. You get the picture.

As I discuss in the introduction of *What If? Writing Exercises for Fiction Writers,* a textbook I co-authored with Anne Bernays, exercises have long been a part of writers' apprenticeship. Hemingway and Fitzgerald wrote letters to each other pointing out "tricks" they had learned from other writers. Fitzgerald names his own teachers in the following passage:

> By style, I mean color . . . I want to be able to do anything with words: handle slashing, flaming descriptions like Wells, and use the paradox with the clarity of Samuel Butler, the breadth of Bernard Shaw and the wit of Oscar Wilde, I want to do the wide sultry heavens of Conrad, the rolled gold sundowns and crazy-quilt skies of Hichens and Kipling as well as pastelle [sic] dawns and twilights of Chesterton. All that is by way of example. As a matter of fact I am a professional literary thief—hot after the best methods of every writer in my generation.

Joan Didion taught herself to write by typing Hemingway's "perfect sentences." Gabriel Garcia-Marquez said upon reading Kafka for the first time, "I didn't know anyone was allowed to write things like that. If I had known, I would have started writing a long time ago. So I immediately started writing."

I tell my students, read Kafka's short short story "The Truth about Sancho Panza" and then borrow a character from a well-known story and write your own story. In Kafka's story, Sancho Panza names his own demon Don Quixote, who then proceeds to go off on his own on the "maddest exploits." Out of a sense of responsibility, Sancho Panza follows him and had of his last days "a great and edifying entertainment." Invariably—and this is true no matter what exercise students begin with—when the stories are discussed in class, the exercise eventually drops away and we consider two things: does the story work and does the last sentence effectively end it?

The short short story workshop lasts four hours and during that time we discuss a short short story by every member of the class. To provide variety, I've added another assignment to the course. Each week, two students create an exercise of their own based on a story they've chosen from the anthology we are using that semester. Cecilia Tan came up with "The Chain Story" based on Francine Prose's story "Pumpkins" from *Flash Fiction*. (My "list" exercise is based on Gregory Burnham's story, "Subtotals," also published in *Flash Fiction*.) Each exercise is composed of two parts: an analysis of the story and directions for using the story as a model for your own story. We discuss these student-generated exercises in terms of understanding and appreciating the story itself, and then addressing the exercise that came from it. When the entire class has presented their exercises, the assignment for the next week is to write a story based on a classmate's exercise.

Once a semester, a workshop is given over entirely to revised stories, though I encourage students to bring in revisions for me to see at any time. I also require students to send out their work to magazines. In fact, all of the stories in *Brevity & Echo* have been published in well-regarded "real world" literary venues, and when Anne Bernays and I revised *What If?* in 2004, we added a section of exercises for the short short story and used published stories by Emerson students to illustrate each exercise.

Happily, there are many short short anthologies from which to assemble a required reading list. Some of my favorites are *Short Shorts: An Anthology of the Shortest Stories,* edited by Irving and Ilana W. Howe, and *Sudden Fiction,* with its lively discussion by forty writers of the short short story form, edited by Robert Shapard and James Thomas. Other *Sudden Fiction* anthologies followed, such as *Flash Fiction,* edited by James Thomas; *Micro Fiction,* edited by Jerome Stern; and *Sudden*

Stories: The Mammoth Book of Miniscule Fiction, edited by Dinty Moore. A new *Flash Fiction Forward* edited by James Thomas and Robert Shapard was published in August 2006. This year, I am also adding two magazines edited by former Emerson students to my list of required texts: *Quick Fiction,* edited by Jennifer Pieroni and Adam Pieroni and *Night Train,* edited by Rusty Barnes and Rod Siino, which runs an annual competition for the short short story titled "Firebox Fiction."

At the end of the semester, each student puts together a collection of short shorts complete with title, table of contents, and flap copy. We are always amazed at how much work everyone has done in one semester.

Can you tell? I love these stories, I love teaching this course. And I am gratified to see all of this fine work together in one impressive volume.

My final words in this Afterword are for two courageous and insightful writers and editors: Congratulations Abigail Beckel and Kathleen Rooney for launching a new press, the wonderfully named Rose Metal Press. And thank you for making *Brevity & Echo* your first published book.

Hinshaw, Brian. "The Custodian." *Sun Dog: The Southeast Review*, Vol. 16, No. 2, 1997; *The Writer's Chronicle*, 33.6, 2001; *What If? Writing Exercises for Fiction Writers* (2nd Edition). Edited by Anne Bernays and Pamela Painter. Longman, 2003.

Cheek, Chip. "Happy Families Are All the Same." *Quick Fiction*, Issue 10, 2006.

Rice, Ashley. "Nebraska." *www.3711Atlantic.com*, April 2005.

Helmuth, Christopher. "Tulip." *The Mississippi Review* (Online), Vol. 9, No. 3, 2003; republished in Vol. 9, No. 4.

Holzer, Amanda. "Love and Other Catastrophes: A Mix Tape." *StoryQuarterly*, Issue 38, 2002; *Best American Non-Required Reading 2003*, Edited by Zadie Smith and Dave Eggers. Houghton Mifflin, 2003.

Avallon, Joanne. "The History You've Been Trying to Write." *Sun Dog: The Southeast Review*, Vol. 15, No. 2/Vol. 16, No. 1, 1996; *Micro Fiction: An Anthology of Fifty* Really *Short Stories*, Edited by Jerome Stern. W.W. Norton & Co., 1996.

Ableman, Derrick. "Games My Father Played." *Swingset Magazine*, Vol. 1, No. 1, 2002; *Dirt Press*, Vol. 1, No. 1, July 2005.

Schneider, Nina R. "Party Favors." *Quick Fiction*, Issue 4, 2003.

O'Hara, Maryanne. "Diverging Paths and All That." *Micro Fiction: An Anthology of Fifty* Really *Short Stories*, Edited by Jerome Stern. W.W. Norton & Co., 1996; *What If? Writing Exercises for Fiction Writers* (2nd Edition). Edited by Anne Bernays and Pamela Painter. Longman, 2003.

Himmer, Steve. "How To Make Potato Salad." *Bullfight*, September 2004.

Robb, Joe. "Gory Joy." *Quick Fiction*, Issue 9, 2006.

Duhamel, Denise. "Casino." *Shade 2006: An Anthology of Poetry and Fiction*, Edited by David Dodd Lee. Four Way Books, 2006.

DeCarteret, Mark. "Baldness." *Quick Fiction,* Issue 6, 2004.

Rittenhouse, Matt. "Funny Things That Happen." *Quick Fiction*, Issue 8, 2005.

Steinberg, R. S. "Fancy Footwork." *New Times*' 20th Annual 55 Fiction Contest Winner, *New Times*, July 2006.

Huffman, Shannon. "Star Light." *Redivider*, Vol. 3, No. 2, 2006.

Busler, Leslie. "Melon." *Salt Hill*, No. 15, Winter 2004.

Ruuska, Braiian. "Buttermelon." *Quick Fiction*, Issue 5, 2004.

Berentson, Jane. "How To Be a Real Ballerina." *Redivider*, Vol. 3, No. 2, 2006.

van den Berg, Laura. "Girl Talk." *StoryQuarterly*, Issue 41, Fall 2005.

Clark, Amy L. "Dear Mr. President." *McSweeney's* Internet Tendency, Gabe Hudson's "Dear Mr. President Letters" August 29, 2005, *www.mcsweeneys.net/letters/president.*

Masih, Tara L. "Out of Africa." *Tall Grasses: Two Fables*. The Feral Press, March 2006.

Royer, Beth Anne. "We Change Our Names." *Quick Fiction*, Issue 8, 2005.

Southwick, Kimberly Ann. "July." *Stork*, Vol. 2, Spring 2005.

Dionne, Erin. "New Rollerskates." *Beacon Street Review*, Vol. 12, No. 2, 1999.

Culbertson, Kirsten. "The Last Word." *Night Train*, Issue 6, 2006.

Masih, Tara L. "Huldi." *The Indian-American*, January 31, 1992.

Himmer, Steve. "A Modern Short Story." *Yankee Pot Roast,* June 2004; *Words!* No. 4, November 2004.

Kersey, John F. "Directions to Minus World." *Directions To Minus World*. Eye For An Iris Press, 2005.

King, Laurel Dile. "Special." *Worcester Magazine*, Vol 29, No. 41, July 1–7, 2004.

Budzko, Stace. "How To Set a House on Fire." *The Southeast Review,* (World's Best Short Short finalist), Vol. 23, No. 2, 2004; *Flash Fiction Forward: 80 Very Short Stories*. Edited by James Thomas and Robert Shapard. W.W. Norton, 2006.

Clark, Amy L. "How To Burn a House." *Quick Fiction*, Issue 9, 2006.

McCracken, Melissa. "Implosion." *New Letters,* Vol. 67, No. 1, 2000.

Pieroni, Jennifer. "Local Woman Gets a Jolt." *Paragraph*, Vol. 8, No. 1, 2002.

Ableman, Derrick. "Reaching Fever." *Dirt Press,* Vol. 1, No. 1, July 2005.

Saliba, Mary. "What I Have to Remember." *Sun Dog: The Southeast Review*, Vol. 13, No. 1, 1993.

French, Elizabeth Kemper. "This Is How I Remember It." *Sundog: The Southeast Review*, Vol. 14, No. 2, 1994; *Micro Fiction: An Anthology of Fifty* Really *Short Stories*, Edited by Jerome Stern. W.W. Norton & Co., 1996; Burroway, Janet. *Imaginative Fiction*. Longman, 2003, 2006.

Rice, Ashley. "The ABCs of Family History." *www.surgeryofmodernwarfare.com*, August 2004.

Marinovich, Matt. "Intelligence." *The Quarterly,* December 1992; *What If? Writing Exercises for Fiction Writers* (2nd Edition). Edited by Anne Bernays and Pamela Painter. Longman, 2003.

O'Leary, Janice. "This Is How We Learned." *Harvard Review*, No. 11, Fall 1996; *Grain*, Vol. 23, No. 3.

Holland, Jacqueline. "Mimi." *Cranky Literary Journal*, Vol. 1, No. 3, September 2004.

Pieroni, Jennifer. "Bad Dog." *Sudden Stories: The Mammoth Book of Miniscule Fiction*, Edited by Dinty W. Moore. Mammoth Books, 2003.

Pahigian, Josh. "Sweeping." *Hawaii Review*, No. 57, Summer 2001.

Lanzarotta, Molly. "One Day Walk Through the Front Door." *What If? Writing Exercises for Fiction Writers* (2nd Edition). Edited by Anne Bernays and Pamela Painter. Longman, 2003.

Himmer, Steve. "Drag." *Insolent Rudder*, August 2004.

Busler, Leslie. "Lovely." *www.pindeldyboz.com*, July 2003.

Ruuska, Braiian. "I Invented the Moonwalk (and the Pencil Sharpener)." *Quick Fiction*, Issue 6, 2004.

Helmuth, Christopher. "Winter." *Green Mountains Review*, Vol. XVIII, No. 1, Fall 2005.

Repino, Robert. "Pictures of Children Playing." *Word Riot,* April 2005.

Quarles, Heather. "A Case for Sterner Prison Sentencing and Reflections on Personal Tragedy By Bear." *The North American Review.*

Lee, Don. "Abercrombie & Fitch." *www.failbetter.com*, Spring 2004.

McGuirk, Sheehan. "Pricks." *What If? Writing Exercises for Fiction Writers* (2nd Edition). Edited by Anne Bernays and Pamela Painter. Longman, 2003.

Masih, Tara L. "Turtle Hunting." *Hayden's Ferry Review*, No. 6, Summer 1990; *Tall Grasses: Two Fables*. The Feral Press, March 2006.

Royer, Beth Anne. "Call Carmine." *Quick Fiction*, Issue 8, 2005.

Carter, Keith Loren. "Bouncing." *Mid-American Review*, Vol. XXII, No. 2, Spring 2002; *Sudden Stories: The Mammoth Book of Miniscule Fiction*, Edited by Dinty W. Moore. Mammoth Press, Inc., 2003.

Duhamel, Denise. "My Mother's Hair." *Gargoyle*, Vol. 50, 2005.

Steinberg, R. S. "A Med School Lesson." read on Boston NPR program *The Connection* on July 24, 1998; NPR website, *www.wgbh.org*, July 1998.

Harrington, Lee. "How To Become a Country-Western Singer." *Sun Dog: The Southeast Review*

Landry, Mariette. "Dancing." *Sun Dog: The Southeast Review*, Vol. 13, No. 1, 1993; *What If? Writing Exercises for Fiction Writers* (2nd Edition). Edited by Anne Bernays and Pamela Painter. Longman, 2003.

Barnes, Rusty. "Love and Murder." *www.smokelong.com*, December 2004; reprinted in *SmokeLong Annual*.

Thuemling, Terry. "ALFALFA." *StoryQuarterly*, Issue 39, 2003; *What If? Writing Exercises for Fiction Writers* (2nd Edition). Edited by Anne Bernays and Pamela Painter. Longman, 2003.

Carr, Jennifer. "Photo by the Bed." *Alaska Quarterly Review*, Fall 2000.

Heller, Jen. "458 Miles through the Texas Panhandle with the Former Love of my Life." *Quick Fiction*, Issue 3, 2003.

McQueen, LaTanya. "How to Cheat (On Your Wife)." *Rumble*, July 2005.

Ruuska, Braiian. "Braggo Roth's Bag o' Broth." *Quick Fiction*, Issue 3, 2003.

Busler, Leslie. "Memoir of a Bookshelf." *Quick Fiction*, Issue 4, 2003.

Rice, Ashley. "Train-Jumping." *www.pindeldyboz.com*, February 2004.

Harrington, Lee. "Oral Fixations." *Sun Dog: The Southeast Review*

Terwilliger, Cam. "An Account of the Life of Doctor Victor Frankenstein." *The GSU Review*, Fall/Winter 2005.

Helmuth, Christopher. "At the Movies." *Third Coast,* Spring 2002.

McCracken, Melissa. "I Always Know It's Over When They Say." *Rag Shock Four*, Lunar Offensive Press, 2003.

Barnes, Rusty. "Death Angels." *www.vistalreview.net*, July 2004.

Carr, Jennifer. "Green Grass: *A Fable*." *Columbia: A Journal of Literature and Art*, Issue 31, Winter 1999.

DERRICK ABLEMAN received his BFA in Writing, Literature and Publishing from Emerson College in 2002. While it may not be obvious to the casual observer, he is trying really, really hard. He thanks you for your time and attention today.

JOANNE AVALLON received her MFA in Creative Writing from Emerson College in 1996. She is a freelance writer currently living in Beverly, Massachusetts.

RUSTY BARNES received his MFA in Creative Writing from Emerson College in 1995, and is the co-founder of *Night Train* (www.nighttrainmagazine.com). His fiction, poetry, and interviews have appeared in many journals. His website is www.rustybarnes.com.

JANE BERENTSON is from western Washington State, where she grew up reading books and working agricultural jobs. She completed the MA in Publishing and Writing program at Emerson College in 2006. Next she will try something in NYC.

STACE BUDZKO received an MFA in Creative Writing in 2004 from Emerson College, where he currently teaches composition and creative writing. He was a finalist for the Raymond Carver Short Story Award as well as the 2006 Richard Yates Short Story Award and World's Best Short-Short Story and has work forthcoming in Norton's *Flash Fiction Forward*. At present, he is working on his first novel.

LESLIE BUSLER received her MFA in Creative Writing from Emerson College in 2003. Her work has appeared in *Quarterly West*, *Salt Hill*, *Quick Fiction*, and *Pindeldyboz* online. She works at Harvard University.

JENNIFER CARR'S fiction and nonfiction have appeared in numerous publications, including *Prairie Schooner, The Nebraska Review, American Literary Review,* and *Poets & Writers*. Her writing company, WORDSource, specializes in bringing the art of storytelling to the commercial marketplace. She graduated from the Emerson College MFA program in 1996. She lives in Western New York with her husband, Shaun, and little girls Sophie and Georgia.

KEITH LOREN CARTER received his MFA in Creative Writing from Emerson College in 2004. His work has previously appeared in the *Mid-American Review* and the *Beacon Street Review*. He is presently working as a sales engineer in the telecommunications industry, where the ability to write fiction is highly valued. He is currently at work on a novel set in Alaska, a number of short stories, and a children's novel that he hopes to finish in time to read to his three children.

CHIP CHEEK will earn his MFA in Creative Writing from Emerson College in May 2007. He is the editor-in-chief of *Redivider* and a fiction reader for *Ploughshares*, and for his day job he works in the college textbook industry. He grew up in Houston and received a degree in journalism from the University of Texas.

AMY L. CLARK is a writer and teacher of writing. She received her BA from Bard College and her MFA in Creative Writing from Emerson College in 2004, where she was awarded the graduate nonfiction prize. She has had several fiction pieces published in literary magazines and is currently working on a novel. She lives in Jamaica Plain, teaches in Cambridge, and works in Boston. Amy has always wanted to be an astronaut.

KIRSTEN CULBERTSON received her MFA in Creative Writing from Emerson College in 1996. Her work has appeared in *Night Train, Pearl, Flashquake,* and the *Philadelphia City Paper*. She is a recipient of Philadelphia's First Person Arts award in memoir and has presented her work at readings in Philadelphia and Los Angeles. She currently lives in Wynnewood, Pennsylvania, and teaches writing at West Chester University.

MARK DECARTERET received his BFA in Creative Writing from Emerson College in 1990. His work has appeared in the anthologies *American Poetry: The Next Generation* (Carnegie Mellon Press, 2000) and *Thus Spake the Corpse: An Exquisite Corpse Reader 1988–1998* (Black Sparrow Press, 2000). His latest chapbook *The Great Apology* was published several years back by Oyster River Press, for which he also co-edited the anthology *Under the Legislature of Stars: 62 New Hampshire Poets*.

ERIN DIONNE received her BA in English and Communications from Boston College and received an MFA in Creative Writing from Emerson College in 1999. Her writing has appeared in *The Boston Globe, The Boston Herald,* and *The HornBook Guide*. Her short fiction has appeared in *Slow Trains Literary Journal, Beacon Street Review,* and the online magazine *Velle.* In March of 2006, she was named one of PEN/New England's Children's Book Caucus Discovery Night honorees.

DENISE DUHAMEL received her BFA in Creative Writing and Literature from Emerson College in 1984. Her poetry titles include *Two and Two* (University of Pittsburgh Press, 2005), *Mille et un Sentiments* (Firewheel, 2005), *Queen for a Day: Selected and New Poems* (Pittsburgh, 2001), *The Star-Spangled Banner* (Southern Illinois University Press, 1999), and *Kinky* (Orchises, 1997). She also edited, with Nick Carbó, *Sweet Jesus: Poems about the Ultimate Icon* (Anthology Press, 2002). She is an associate professor, teaching poetry at Florida International University in Miami.

ELIZABETH KEMPER FRENCH received her MFA in Creative Writing from Emerson College in 1996. Her stories have appeared in *The North American Review, StoryQuarterly, Sundog: The Southeast Review,* and *Ploughshares,* and her work has been reprinted in the anthology *Micro Fiction* (Norton, 1996) and *Imaginative Fiction* (Longman, 2003). She received special mentions in Pushcart Prize XXIII and *Best American Short Stories, 2002.* She lives on the southern coast of Massachusetts with her husband and daughter, where she teaches writing and is at work on a novel.

LEE HARRINGTON received her MFA in Creative Writing from Emerson College in 1997. She is the author of the best-selling memoir *Rex and the City: a Woman, a Man, and a Dysfunctional Dog* (Villard, 2006). Her novel, *Nothing Keeps a Frenchman from His Lunch* will be published by Random House in 2007.

JEN HELLER received her BFA in Writing, Literature and Publishing from Emerson College in 2001. She has been published in multiple issues of *Quick Fiction* and has appeared in *Round Magazine*, *The Emerson Review*, and *Straight Magazine*. Her work is also forthcoming in a fiction anthology by Eye for an Iris Press. She and her husband live happily in Austin, Texas, where they enjoy great live music in their spare time.

CHRISTOPHER HELMUTH received his MFA in Creative Writing from Emerson College in 2002. Originally from Carlisle, Pennsylvania, he currently lives in Boston, where he works at the Harvard School of Public Health. His stories have appeared in or are forthcoming from *The Greensboro Review*, *Ascent*, *The Florida Review*, *The Mississippi Review* (Online), *Third Coast*, and *Green Mountains Review*, among others.

STEVE HIMMER received his MFA in Creative Writing from Emerson College in 2005. He lives near Boston with his wife and dog.

BRIAN HINSHAW received his MFA in Creative Writing from Emerson College in 1997. He teaches at the University of Wisconsin-Milwaukee. His work has appeared in *Sun Dog: The Southeast Review*, *The Potomac Review*, *The Village Ramble*, and *What If?* He is at work on a novel, but still hasn't received the oranges.

JACQUELINE HOLLAND received her MA in Publishing and Writing from Emerson College in 2004. She hails from Watertown, Massachusetts, where she spends a lot of time thinking about writing while managing to write very little, thus finding the short short genre a brilliant one. She is fond of yard sales, low tide, and long-haired dachshunds.

AMANDA HOLZER received her BFA in Writing, Literature and Publishing from Emerson College in 2002.

SHANNON HUFFMAN received her MFA in Creative Writing from Emerson College in May 2006. Her work has been published in *Redivider*, *Quick Fiction*, and *Pearl*. To make money, she has written obituaries, delivered pizza, and sold industrial-strength cleaner door to door. She lives in Ossipee, New Hampshire, with her husband Bill and four misbehaved cats.

JOHN F. KERSEY received his BFA in Writing, Literature and Publishing from Emerson in 2002. He was born in New Hampshire. Currently he lives either there or in Asheville, North Carolina, where he works on various artistic and literary projects. In his brief life he has toured with Boston's Guerilla Poets, taught high school English, incorporated and co-edited for Eye For An Iris Press (based in Brooklyn, NY), and broken several bones in his body. He has occasionally had the pleasure of seeing his work published.

LAUREL DILE KING received her MFA in Creative Writing from Emerson College in 2001. She is the recipient of a Massachusetts Cultural Council Artists' Grant and the winner of the 2004 *Worcester Magazine* Short Story Contest. She teaches short fiction and the novel at the Worcester Art Museum. Her first published short story was in the *Beacon Street Review*. She is currently at work on a novel and lives in Shrewsbury with her husband and two sons.

REBECCA KRZYZANIAK received an MA in Writing and Publishing from Emerson College in 2004 with an emphasis in book design and production, but not before developing a feverish affinity for playing with lead type and printing on old letterpresses. Rebecca held various artistic production positions with the *Atlantic Monthly*, Houghton Mifflin, and Allyn & Bacon in the Boston area before venturing south to Florida where she spent weekends on the beach and weekdays cranking out magazine pages for a local city mag *SRQ*. She has returned from Florida's Gulf coast and can be found peering out her Waltham window when procrastinating on freelance work or preparing for the desktop publishing course she teaches at Emerson.

MARIETTE LANDRY received her MFA in Creative Writing from Emerson College in 1991. Her work has appeared in *Poetry East*, *Indiana Review*, *Compost*, and *The North American Review*, as well as in the anthology *Micro Fiction* (Norton, 1996). She received an AWP Intro Journals Prize as an Emerson student and a Massachusetts Cultural Council Artists' Grant in poetry. She has taught at Emerson, Northeastern, and Boston University, and currently works with student-athletes at Boston College. She and her husband, Emerson graduate Steve Landry, live in Boston.

MOLLY LANZAROTTA received her MA in Publishing and Writing from Emerson College in 1990. Her short fiction has appeared in publications including the *Cimmaron Review*, *Carolina Quarterly*, *Sun Dog*, and the book *What If?* She also writes essays and plays and has worked as a communications consultant for nonprofit organizations and as a communications specialist in higher ed.

DON LEE received his MFA in Creative Writing from Emerson College in 1987. He is the author of the novel *Country of Origin*, which won an American Book Award, and the short story collection *Yellow*, which won the Sue Kaufman Prize for First Fiction. He is the editor of the literary journal *Ploughshares* and lives in Cambridge, Massachusetts.

MATT MARINOVICH received his MFA in Creative Writing from Emerson College in 1992. His work has appeared in *The Mississippi Review*, *Open City*, *The Quarterly*, *Sonora Review*, *Salon.com*, and other magazines. His novel *Strange Skies* will be published by Harper Perennial in fall 2007.

TARA L. MASIH received her MA in Professional Writing, Literature and Publishing in 1986. She has published fiction, poetry, and essays in numerous anthologies and literary magazines (*Confrontation*, *Hayden's Ferry Review*, *Natural Bridge*, *New Millennium Writings*, *Red River Review*, and *The Caribbean Writer*); her essays have been read on NPR. Two limited edition black-and-white illustrated pamphlets featuring her flash fiction have been published by The Feral Press (Oyster Bay, NY). Her flash fiction has won awards and been nominated for a Pushcart Prize. Her website is www.TaraMasih.com.

MELISSA MCCRACKEN received her MFA in Creative Writing from Emerson College in 2002. She lives in beautiful Santa Fe, New Mexico, where, by day, she runs her own business consulting firm. She is a closet fiction writer the rest of the time and still harbors delusions of publishing books and selling screenplays.

SHEEHAN MCGUIRK received her BFA in Writing, Literature and Publishing from Emerson College in 2000. She is looking for a new job, one that is fairly easy, extremely creative, and high paying. She likes her neighborhood in Brooklyn, New York, French cuisine, Third World lovers, and making birdnests. Sheehan asked me to ask you, "Is this what people do?"

LATANYA MCQUEEN received her BFA in Writing, Literature and Publishing from Emerson College in 2006. Besides *Rumble*, her work has appeared in *Flash Forward*.

MARYANNE O'HARA received her MFA in Creative Writing from Emerson College in 1995. She has published stories in *Five Points*, The *North American Review*, *The Crescent Review*, *Redbook*, and *Micro Fiction*. Her stories have been short listed for the Pushcart Prize and her writing has won some grants in Massachusetts. She is the Associate Fiction Editor of *Ploughshares* and is completing *The End of the Ice Age*, a novel about life during the interwar years.

JANICE O'LEARY received her MFA in Creative Writing from Emerson College in 1996. She is a freelance writer in Boston and an editor at Harvard Medical School. She teaches journalism at Boston University.

JOSH PAHIGIAN is a 2001 graduate of the Emerson College MFA program in Creative Writing. He teaches writing at the University of New England. He has three published books about baseball and two forthcoming books under contract with publishers.

JENNIFER PIERONI received her BFA in Writing, Literature and Publishing from Emerson College in 2001. She is editor-in-chief of *Quick Fiction*.

HEATHER QUARLES received her MFA in Creative Writing from Emerson College in 1996.

ROBERT REPINO spent most of his life in Drexel Hill, Pennsylvania. After serving in the Peace Corps, he moved to Boston and received an MFA in Creative Writing from Emerson College in 2006. His work has appeared in *Word Riot*, *The Furnace Review*, and *'a-pos-tro-phe*. When asked why he writes, he still thinks it's funny to say that writing is the second-most fun a person can have by himself.

ASHLEY RICE received an MFA in Creative Writing from Emerson College in 2004. She is the author and illustrator of several poetry books including *Girls Rule*, *You Are an Amazing Girl*, and *Thanks for Being My Friend*. She lives in Texas.

MATT RITTENHOUSE received his BFA in Writing, Literature and Publishing from Emerson College in 2003. He has had work published in *Quick Fiction*, *One Thousand Ridiculous Tragedies*, and *Scissorpress*. He mostly lives and writes in New Hampshire.

JOE ROBB received an MFA in Creative Writing from Emerson College in 2006. He now lives in Brooksville, Maine and has yet to become sick of the burbling.

BETH ANNE ROYER received her BFA in Writing, Literature and Publishing from Emerson College in 2001. She lives in Connecticut, is pursuing a master's degree in librarianship, enjoys book arts, bicycles, cool nights, and good dogs. In 2004, Slipstream Press published a chapbook of her poems called *Radio Dreams*. She sells crafts at www.threedogparty.com, had artist's books in the 2005 mobilibre exhibition, and her code name is Beverly Writer. In her free time, she teaches memoir writing to senior citizens and tries to build a better apron.

BRAIIAN RUUSKA received his MFA in Creative Writing from Emerson College in 2003. Braiian and his helper-monkey, Mr.

Snakko, can be found at Boston area bus stops, making sure the buses leave on time. Sometimes they don't, so Braiian sternly shakes his fist while Mr. Snakko screeches and points to his comically oversized wristwatch. It seems to help.

MARY SALIBA received her MFA in Creative Writing from Emerson College in 1993. She is the editor of *The Granite State News* and *The Baysider*, both based in Wolfeboro, New Hampshire. A graduate of NYU's Tisch School of the Arts and The Professional Children's School, NY, NY. she wrote for the *New York Daily News* and other publications in NYC. She is currently finishing a book of short stories and a book of poems.

CARRIE SCANGA received her training from Bryn Mawr College (BA) and from the University of Washington (MFA). She has recently exhibited her work at El Conteiner Gallery in Quito, Ecuador, the International Print Center New York, Artspace in Raleigh, North Carolina, and the Islip Art Museum on Long Island. She has been a resident at The MacDowell Colony and Sculpture Space, and in 2004 she received a New York Foundation for the Arts Fellowship. She recently completed two fellowships at the Fine Arts Work Center in Provincetown, and she currently lives in Baton Rouge, where she is the Professional in Residence at Louisiana State University.

NINA R. SCHNEIDER received her MFA in Creative Writing from Emerson College in 2004. She currently teaches writing at Bentley College, in Waltham, Massachusetts, and is working on short fiction. She is an active member of Grub Street, Inc. Her short fiction has appeared in Pindeldyboz.com and Quick Fiction, and she was a finalist in the Moment Magazine Short Fiction Contest 2004.

KIMBERLY ANN SOUTHWICK received her BFA in Writing, Literature and Publishing from Emerson College in 2006. She recommends that you: take as many pictures of the house you grew up in before your parents sell it; listen to Jay-Z and Shoney Lamar; break grammar rules with style; and never forget to send handwritten thank-yous to people you appreciate. Her writing and photography have appeared in *The Emerson Review*, *Gangsters in Concrete*, and *Stork Magazine*. Her photography has also appeared in *The Weekly Dig*.

R. S. STEINBERG received his MFA in Creative Writing from Emerson College in 2001. He started writing fiction after an accident ended his career as an orthopaedic surgeon. His work has been published in *Fiction*, *Bananafish*, and elsewhere.

CAM TERWILLIGER will earn his MFA in Creative Writing from Emerson College in 2007. He is a poet, short story writer, and occasional journalist living in Brookline, Massachusetts. His is the poetry editor for the magazine *Redivider*. Cam spends most of his time working on a book of short stories entitled, *The Zoo in Winter*.

TERRY THUEMLING received his MFA in Creative Writing from Emerson College in 2003. He lives in Milwaukee, Wisconsin, with his wife Rachel and his daughter Esmé. He works at the University of Wisconsin-Milwaukee, where he teaches a variety of writing courses.

LAURA VAN DEN BERG lives in Boston will earn her MFA in Creative Writing in 2008 from Emerson College, where she is a writing instructor and the assistant fiction editor of *Redivider*. Her stories have been published or are forthcoming in *Literary Imagination*, *The Northwest Review*, *The Baltimore Review*, *Third Coast*, *The Greensboro Review*, and *StoryQuarterly*. Her fiction has been nominated for Best New American Voices and was recently a finalist for the Howard Frank Mosher Prize. She is currently at work on a collection of stories.

ABIGAIL BECKEL is a founding publisher of Rose Metal Press, Inc. She has worked professionally in publishing for more than six years, at publishing houses such as Pearson Education and Beacon Press, and currently works for Blackwell Publishing. Her poems have appeared recently in *Rainbow Curve* and *Family Matters: Poems of Our Families* (Bottom Dog Press, 2005). She received her MA in Publishing and Writing from Emerson College in 2005.

KATHLEEN ROONEY is a founding publisher of Rose Metal Press, Inc. She is the author of *Reading With Oprah* (2005), and her poems have appeared recently in *AGNI On-line, Harvard Review, Smartish Pace, Melancholia's Tremulous Dreadlocks,* and *Crab Orchard Review*. Her essay "Live Nude Girl" appears in *Twentysomething Essays by Twentysomething Writers* (Random House, 2006), and her criticism has appeared in *The Nation* and *Boston Review*. She received her MFA in Creative Writing from Emerson College in 2005.

RON CARLSON is the author of eight books of fiction, most recently his selected stories *A Kind of Flying* (W.W. Norton); his new novel *Five Skies* will be published in 2007. His short stories have appeared in *Esquire, Harper's, The New Yorker, Gentlemen's Quarterly, Epoch, The North American Review*, and other journals, as well as *The Best American Short Stories, The O. Henry Prize Series, The Pushcart Prize Anthology, The Norton Anthology of Short Fiction,* and dozens of other anthologies. He teaches fiction writing at UC Irvine.

PAMELA PAINTER is the author of the award-winning story collection, *Getting to Know the Weather*, and of a recent collection titled *The Long and Short of It*. She is also the co-author of the widely-used textbook, *What If? Writing Exercises for Fiction Writers.* Her stories have appeared in *The Atlantic*, *Harper's*, *Kenyon Review*, *Mid-American Review*, *Night Train*, *Ploughshares*, and *Quick Fiction*, among others. Painter's stories have also been reprinted in the short short anthologies, *Sudden Fiction*, *Flash Fiction*, *Micro Fiction*, *Sudden Stories*, and most recently in *Flash Fiction Forward* and *Best American Flash Fiction of the 21st Century*. She lives in Boston and teaches in the Writing, Literature and Publishing Program at Emerson College.

The interior of *Brevity & Echo* is set in Linotype Granjon. George Williams Jones created Granjon for English Linotype in 1924, during a period in which many classic typefaces were being revived and recut. His typeface was called Granjon in honor of the sixteenth-century French printer and type founder, Robert Granjon. However, Jones' Granjon more closely relates to, and is perhaps still the most accurate representation of, an original Claude Garamond (contemporary to Granjon during the French Renaissance) type and was so named in order to differentiate it from the abundance of other Garamond revivals being produced during the late nineteenth and early twentieth centuries. Granjon roman and italic are used for text, with small caps used for titling and in the folio.

The cover of *Brevity & Echo* utilizes the contrasting, yet comparably humanistic, decorative typeface Champleve, digitized by Bill Horton in 1993, with Martin Majoor's sans serif phenom Scala Sans. Champleve can be historically traced back to the early twentieth-century designs of the Parisian Bernard Naudin, while Scala Sans, partner to Majoor's 1990 Serif version, completes the Scala family, which stands alone as a singular, contemporary creation.

Rebecca Krzyzaniak